Revenge! It was a sad tale I had to write, and it all began when I shot the man I loved as a brother. Or did it? Maybe it was when the Black Widow stepped down from the train in Abilene. She wasn't a black widow then, just a very handsome young woman. She destroyed my life, my hopes and the trust of my foster father, as well as losing me my best friend to my own gun. She took my life and happiness, but in the end she paid, and in doing so, gave me something I never hoped to have.

# BLACK WIDOW

# BLACK WIDOW

*by*

Newton Ketton

**Dales Large Print Books**
Long Preston, North Yorkshire,
BD23 4ND, England.

British Library Cataloguing in Publication Data.

---

Ketton, Newton
Black widow.

A catalogue record of this book is available from the British Library

ISBN 978-1-84262-535-4 pbk

First published in Great Britain in 1994 by Robert Hale Limited



Published in Large Print 2007 by arrangement with Robert Hale Ltd.



Dales Large Print is an imprint of Library Magna Books Ltd.

Printed and bound in Great Britain by
T.J. (International) Ltd., Cornwall, PL28 8RW

For Reg,
A maddening, stubborn, rumbustious
cowboy, who liked his pint
and was quite a guy.

# ONE

The day I blasted my pard, Jed Coggins, was the day that sliced my life into two parts, the before and the after. Yes, sir! I've always regarded that day as the abyss that divided the boy from the man. And it was all because of a woman. Kate Beamish.

It's been nigh on forty years and yet I can still see the trim waist, luscious hips and the laughing Irish eyes of her, not to mention neat ankles and bosoms a man would give his last dollar to handle.

Yes, sir! She was some woman! And I never even got to taste her rosy lips or smell the real womanliness of her and for why? Because the bitch set me up and I narrowly missed my own hanging by a whisker.

And that, believe me or not, was because of another little filly called Bonny Bluefeathers who had a notion for me and didn't mind messing with the sheriff's deputy the night before I was to swing. She fooled him proper. Let him have his way and then got him drunk and swiped his keys. I didn't even stop to kiss her goodbye...

I left with hate in my heart for Kate Beamish. I couldn't risk hanging around to catch her coming out of the Longhorn but I vowed to get her some day...

Me and Jed were good buddies. We'd survived some hairy times together during the Civil War and saved each other's lives a couple of times so we were closer than brothers.

We loved each other did Jed and me and when we scrapped, we stood back to back and dished out hell to whoever come up against us. We knew what each of us was a'doing. No need to watch cross-eyed. It all came natural-like and so we watched each other's backs, and we didn't need eyes in our arses.

We were in the middle of a brawl in the

Longhorn Saloon in Abilene. I'd just knocked a feller over the bar with a bone-jarring clout that nearly broke my fist. It stung some. Jed had just given Shaggy Cotton a stinger and was lifting him up to chuck him through the window, when he paused and dropped Shaggy on his head slap bang on the floor. He groaned and lay still.

I was blowing on my knuckles and I looked towards the wooden staircase where Jed was looking, all bug-eyed.

'Chre-ist! Do you see what I see?' he gagged, and all hell melted out of him leaving him weak and soppy-looking.

I spat on the floor, still full of piss and vinegar and raring to go, but what with Shaggy snoring his fool head off and his pard Dicky Jones, all tangled up behind the bar and Sammy the swamper slapping him to bring him round, there was no one willing to take me on, that is, no one without sense.

Me and Jed were famous for our Saturday night set-to's when we got loaded up with rotgut. We didn't enjoy Saturday night unless there was a bust-up before we went upstairs to get our bruises fixed up by Molly or Bonny or the little redhead, Annie-May and so I wasn't very quick off the mark when I looked at the vision of eastern loveliness. Indeed, I was a bit mad with Jed being so soppy.

'Yeh, I see her. Must have come in on the stage.'

Jed never even heard my reply but strode straight over to her like an arrow from a bow. He didn't even give her time to spit.

'Howdy, miss, and what might your name be?'

She looked him up and down as if she had a stink under her nose. She was like some black-haired duchess all frilled up in emerald green satin and black lace, a fetching piece when I got a good look at her without the blood pounding in my ears.

She must have liked what she saw for she smiled, showing even white teeth and extended her hand, polite-like and Jed, stupid fool, bent over it like some mountebank courtier and damn me, if he didn't kiss it! I wanted to puke!

'Kate ... Kate Beamish, but you can call me Kate.' She fluttered her cow eyes and Jed was lost. That was the moment when I lost Jed. Never before had a woman come between us. 'And who might I be talking to?' she asked, all coy and come-onish.

'Jed Coggins of the Bar C ranch and this is my pard, Lofty Williams.' Jed motioned me over and I unstuck my feet and wandered across. Her hand was soft. She'd washed no dishes all right. I didn't kiss it and I think she knew that I hadn't fallen under no spell. She raised a fine black eyebrow and looked me up and down and I tried to straighten my gangly frame. I didn't carry no beef in those days and I suppose I looked what I was, a rough tough cowboy whose pard's old man ran one of the most successful ranches south of Abilene.

Old Coggins was a shrewd old buzzard. He met the oncoming herds on the trail to

Abilene and bought 'em cheap from tired trail-bosses and fattened 'em up a spell and then off-loaded 'em quick back east without the hassle of driving 'em up to the stock-yards. Yessir! Old Coggins had more brain in his little finger than Jed had in his whole body, with me included.

It seems the little lady had heard the name Coggins, for her eyes flashed again at Jed and apart from giving me her hand, ignored me completely.

'May I clean up that cut for you?' She put a gentle hand on his cheek. The whole damn saloon saw him quiver. I wanted to slap her down.

'Would you? You're being very kind,' and that fool feller followed her upstairs like a bloody lamb to the slaughter!

She never seemed to notice that I was suffering a far bloodier wound than Jed was and I ground my teeth in a rage. I couldn't understand it for I didn't like her or her kind. I knew instinctively that she was one who liked a deep pocket in a man's trousers and that her greedy little fist had free access.

Bonny touched me on the arm and with an effort I turned and smiled at her. Her eyes showed concern. They were pretty eyes too, dark and liquid and were the finest feature in her round placid face.

'Let me clean you up. We'll go upstairs.'

I nodded. This was something that happened every Saturday night. Bonny cleaned me up, bandaged any cuts, put some Indian concoction on my bruises and then boosted my ego in bed.

She was a good kid and never jawed my ear or expected anything more than a Saturday night tumble. She got regular dollars and I let off steam as a man should and then, along with Jed, we went back to the weekly business of punching ornery cows.

This time it was different. There was something to talk about.

'What's this Kate doing here? I didn't think Charlie Emmerson would lash out on a fancy piece like her. She'll be too rich for Charlie's pocket.'

Bonny worked quickly on the gash in my bonce cutting away a bit of hair which I couldn't afford to lose as it was going without my help. She laughed, showing the gap between her teeth where one had been knocked out by a drunken punter who'd blamed her for not being able to get it up.

'Don't be fooled by the clothes, Lofty. She's broke, and she's looking around for a new nest.'

'So she's not aiming to stay and work in the saloon?'

I was conscious of regret. Something in me was attracted to the bitch. I suppose it would have been nice and a special experience to lie beside some sweet-smelling body like hers, especially if she was up to some of them there tricks I'd heard about from the fellers in the saloon. Eastern women were supposed to be full of different ways of getting a reluctant pecker up and doing. Whiskey was always hell on a man's willingness to perform. Usually the girls didn't care: All they wanted was the dough.

But girls from back east liked their pleasure too, or so it was said, and Kate Beamish looked as if she picked and chose her men for their performance, and she'd picked a good 'un in Jed. He could usually come up with the goods even if it took him all night.

'No. She's staying here because she knew Charlie from way back. I have a feeling she's targeting someone. I don't know who. I was listening at her bedroom door when she first arrived. Charlie was with her and I was wondering whether the old goat was taking out the rent in the usual way. But he wasn't, which was surprising knowing him. They was talking low and serious and I heard her tell him she'd been thrown out after five years and all she had to show for it was a couple of portmanteaus of clothes, a few cheap jewels and a thousand dollars and she needed a new man quite smartish.'

'And then what?'

'They talked some more and I heard Charlie laugh and he bet her that someone I couldn't hear the name of, wouldn't buy it.

That he was a cautious cuss and didn't let his left hand know what his right hand was doing. She took him on and what do you know?'

Irritated, I shook my head.

'How the hell do I know? Go on, you're dying to tell me.'

'Well, she bet him a thousand dollars! What d'you think about that?'

'She's either a fool or a good gambler, or she's damn sure of herself. I wonder who she's after?'

But Bonny was getting bored and her hands were now running all over me. My gashed head was throbbing dully but it wasn't slowing up my reactions any.

Suddenly Kate Beamish wasn't important any more. Bonny was lying beside me, keen and eager to please. I snuggled up to her warm sweaty body savouring the scent of her and I went off at a gallop. But somewhere inside me, I could smell and taste that damned woman. Bonny would have stuck a knife in my ribs if she'd known I was pretending she was Kate....

I still couldn't understand it as I rode back to the ranch with Jed that cool spring Sunday morning. Neither of us spoke of the night's adventures. I glanced at him but he was riding all thoughtful and staring straight between his horse's ears.

I wanted to ask him if all they said about eastern women was true but something about him stopped me. No doubt he would tell me later. We often compared notes and I didn't think this would be any different.

But Jed surprised me. Later, when we arrived back and corraled the horses and fed and watered them and Jed was heaving his saddle on to one of the saddlehorses to air off, I put a tentative question.

'Well? How was it?'

He gave me a long level look and ignored the question and strode indoors. His feet rattled sharply on the boards. I followed and was just in time to see old Coggins look up from the Bible he was reading from, and frown.

'You're late, both of you.' He gave both Jed and myself a scowling going-over, noting the bandages and bruises. He never could understand that to young fellers back from the excitement of the war, we had to rid ourselves of all that aggression that accumulated all week in a good old punch-up. We enjoyed coming back limping and aching and released from tension.

We also enjoyed the afterwards, when Charlie's girls tended us and pampered us and gave us what we wanted....

Jed nodded.

'Yeh, something came up...'

'I bet it did!' the old man said with unconscious humour. I wanted to snigger but thought better of it. He had a rumbustious temper for an old man. Fire first and then ask questions, one of those kind.

He'd been good to me from the day I came home with Jed, all shot up and shellshocked so that I was all of a twitch. He said he'd fatten me up but he never did of course. I was always a tall gangly feller with a long narrow face and looking as if I didn't know how to smile, which was a bit off-putting to the girls, except for Bonny who knew different. I smiled inside, and she said I was quite entertaining when I let myself go. But then, anyone can let go when they're full of rotgut and the ghosts of dead comrades is laid to rest for a little while.

I perked up and pricked my ears when Jed said a bit hesitantly for him,

'Pa, how'd you fancy having a real classy housekeeper? Someone who'd chivvy old Lola around and turn this damned pigsty into a real home?'

The old man closed the Bible with a snap and leaned back in the old wheelback chair and considered Jed who was now looking decidedly uncomfortable and I realized for the first time, that as old as he was and an ex-soldier to boot, he still regarded his old man with the same awe as he had done as a shaver. It rather tickled my sense of humour. I filed the fact away to trot out at a later date when I wanted to rile him.

'Now what's bugging you, Jed? Since when has it bothered you that we live in a pigsty?'

Jed shrugged.

'I'm coming up thirty, Pa. We should be getting the place fixed. I might want to bring a wife home and how could I with the place looking like this; horse shit on the floor, straw in the corners and harness all over the place and not a decent seat to sit on. Just look at it, Pa.'

Both me and old Coggins looked about. The place was certainly a mess but everything was to hand. Rifles at the ready, boots and bullwhips and branding irons ready where they could be found in a hurry. The big table that seated us three and the other cowboys was reasonably clean and was always scrubbed by Lola at least once a week. The benches too, were slopped over occasionally when someone's arse had come in contact with some cow shit.

I didn't care how it looked. The fat black-bellied stove gave out heat and Lola fed us stew and fresh bread and the smell of that drowned out the other smells. She didn't nag us about dirty boots or spitting on the floor. I thought it a pretty good set-up.

The old man thought it was too.

'Have you some high-falutin' piece in mind, boy?'

Jed shuffled his feet and looked a fool.

'Not yet, Pa, but it has crossed my mind...'

'Only just,' said old Coggins sagely. 'It's only last week you were threatening to move out taking Lofty here, with you, but you changed your mind damned fast when I told you to bugger off and not come back!'

'Aw hell! That was just a load of bullshit. We was bored, weren't we, Lofty?' And I dutifully nodded. He went on, 'So how about it, Pa? Do you fancy a good-class housekeeper?'

'Is she the one who's took your fancy? You want to try her out here?'

'Well now, I hadn't thought of that, but it might come to it. She's a high-class respect-able lady and we should be going up in the world, Pa. If you put your mind to it, you could be someone in Abilene, instead of rusting away out here and only counting the dollars.'

'Sounds to me as if you're repeating someone else's words, son.'

I thought so too, and I knew who it was. The bitch had lost no time in feeding Jed all the old crap about improving himself and how she could help him do it. I wondered what she'd said about me. I could bet my last buck that she would suggest giving me the old heave-ho and that I was just a bloody leech hanging in there and hoping to get a stake in the ranch when the old man snuffed it. I did think that, I must admit, for the old man treated me like another son and I'd worked hard and long for him.

Jed looked sulky.

'Look, Pa, the words were said but they were only what I've been thinking a long time...' Liar I thought, you didn't have the brain to work that lot out and if you had, you would have talked to me about it... The old man's look coincided with what I was thinking. He drummed his fingers on the table and then looked about him again. Then he sighed heavily.

'Your ma would never have let this place go, God rest her! Maybe you're right. Not that I want to kick up in Abilene. I want no truck with them thieving devils! But maybe I should think of the future and you and Lofty here and the ranch. Maybe it's time to work things out. I'm not going to live for ever!'

'Hell, Pa! I wasn't for meaning that you was past it! I just wanted to give Miss Beamish the offer of a home. She's a destitute lady with a need for some place secure, and where some respect would be shown to her.'

Suddenly old Coggins grinned.

'You sure sound smitten, boy. I never heard tell of you respecting no woman before. So you want to court her all proper, do you?'

'Sure, Pa, if she would have me. I think I could live in double harness with a woman of her breeding. I could even give up my

Saturday nights...' I groaned inwardly ... Jesus, he must have got it bad or else she'd been a helluva tigress in bed!

'You make me curious about her, Jed. What about asking her to stay for a coupla weeks and see how she pans out?'

Jed looked hastily around and said quickly, 'We'll have to help Lola fix this place up and clear out the tack. Lofty, you're good at rooting out things in the store; you could get some fixin's like an Indian rug to cover the scarred floor and some curtains and maybe some new pots and pans. You know the drill!'

I was a bit took aback. By hell, he was serious about her and I cursed. She was going to be like an ongoing canker to him. She was going to grow on him, and I had a premonition nothing would ever be the same again ... I was going to be pushed out. If she managed to hook him, then she would make sure there were kids and Lofty Williams wouldn't get a look in. I might as well get on my horse now and ride out into the sunset and save myself some hassle.

How I wished I had. How I cursed myself for not listening to that intuition that had got me out of scrapes during the war.

It would have saved me from a lifetime of regret…

## TWO

Kate's arrival at the Bar C was like a bolt of lightning. Everyone was affected, from Lola who detested her on sight, to the cowhands who couldn't think of enough excuses to come to the back door, knock, and leer at her as they asked for sewing needles or thread or if she had ointment for their cuts which before she arrived, they spat on and forgot about.

They talked about her incessantly in the bunk-house and Scufter Bingham, who had a way with words, made 'em all edgy with his salacious suggestions of what he might do with her if he got the chance.

It got so bad that even I got rattled and snuck off to see Bonny in the middle of the week and then found she wasn't available. She was entertaining some cattle buyer from out of town.

I blamed Kate Beamish for being at the ranch and giving Scufter itches in his breeches and then passing them on to me so that I found out that Bonny was no better than she oughter be. It was hell and I didn't like it although I knew she had to make her living the best way she could. Charlie was no Good Samaritan and would have turfed her out if she didn't come up with the rent for using his room as 'business premises'.

Anyhow, there was a fine old howdydo and only Jed was going around with a grin on his chops and a lewd song on his lips.

Old Coggins was more surly than ever and that should have been a kinda warning if I'd had the wit to see it. But I didn't and so had no way of knowing how the land was lying...

Then Kate started complaining about Scufter eyeing her up and following her about when he wasn't out punching cows. Got real pally with me and I was flattered. She said she knew how much I thought of Jed and she didn't want to worry him about the business with Scufter as he had a temper like his Pa's if things didn't go right, and she couldn't bear arguments and bloodshed and would never forgive herself if anyone fought over her...

Believe me, I was dumbstruck. I never guessed her to be sensitive or weak-gutted. I'd sized her up as a mean, tough lady and now she was giving me the soft doe-eyed look, murmuring things like me being so strong and the kind to lean on, and giving me little hints about if it wasn't for hurting Jed, she could get real hung up on me... Yeah, and I fell for it, didn't I?

She was a bloody good manipulator and I should have known better, since I'd figured her from the beginning as being what she really was.

I should have slapped her down that very first night.

I certainly should have shook my brains up and come up with a way of showing her up in her true colours.

But I didn't, did I? I was just a thick, bumbling cowboy who was suspicious of her but still fool enough to believe that silvery Irish tongue of hers. I was open to flattery and the bitch knew it!

She was manipulating us all, even poor old Lola got so that she took on all the menial tasks while Kate played the lady!

I realized too late that she was also dazzling Scufter with her hellish hints and playing him like a fish, pulling him in and then letting him out so that the poor bastard didn't know whether he was coming or going.

And all the time this was going on, no one noticed the effect on old man Coggins.

True, he'd spruced up. Took a bath every coupla weeks when he used to settle for one every two-three months depending what mucky job he'd been doing. He bought a store suit and a new hat that looked ridiculous on him and Kate ironed his shirts herself and made him change 'em every week.

Oh, yes, Kate made a difference to old Tom

Coggins and Jed and me were two blind bats and never suspected a thing. Poor old Jed never did see. He thought he was doing all the courting around the Bar C. But events proved different though Jed wasn't around to see the final outcome.

I found Kate crying one day down beside the well. The wooden bucket was tossed into a cactus thicket and her bodice was torn and there were scratches on one round white bosom.

Me, like the fool I was, jumped in with both feet.

'Kate! What's going on here?' And before I could reason things out I was picking her up from the dirt and holding her close. She looked up to me with those soft doe eyes and I was floored what with the feel of her quivering body and the right good smell of her.

'Lofty,' she breathed, and tears spilled from her eyes like a mountain stream in full spate. 'It's that Scufter. He was trying ... you know.' She bit her underlip real prettily. I could have murdered the bastard if he had been anywhere in sight.

Mind you, later on, I was a bit puzzled for I remembered Jed telling him to go to the far pastures with old Docherty to look for strays. He couldn't have been in two places at once, but at the time I was thinking of her warm body clamped tight against mine and telling me things in right contrast to what her mouth was saying.

I comforted her right well, too well, for suddenly she was pulling me down on the ground and I'll admit I didn't shy away from what she was doing.

It hit me suddenly and ferociously and the only excuse I had was that it was a Friday and tomorrow night I would have been with Bonny and so Kate got all the pent-up passion that should have been Bonny's.

She couldn't have stopped me if she'd tried. But she didn't and I found out that girls from the east certainly learned different things to make a man wild.

Afterwards, while I lay back exhausted and

heart pounding I saw her watching me with a half-smile on her lips. Now I know she was thinking she had me hooked like the rest. As a matter of fact she had.

I could only think of her as the softest armful, bar none, that I'd ever been with, bar none, and she beat poor Bonny into a cocked hat. Mind you, Bonny was good when she was in the mood for it but most of the time she was just earning her rent.

I turned over on to my stomach so that I could look at her. Her hand caressed my jaw and she pulled at my whiskers.

'Why now?' I asked her softly. I was calf-sick, half shagged out and half on the rise again. I knew that in ten minutes I'd be a raving bull for the second time in less than half an hour.

I wisht I could tell the boys down in the saloon how it had been. It beat drinking whiskey any day!

I grew bold and she allowed my hand to wander and her skin was as smooth as satin against my calloused hand. She shrugged.

'I like a challenge. I could see it in your eyes. You wanted me.'

'Did I?' That was news to me. I thought I hated her for coming between Jed and me. These days we didn't go rollicking around, getting drunk and into fights. He was always thinking of something else when we talked together.

I knew she attracted me, but I despised her, or did I? Maybe I only thought I did. Anyhow, I liked what she dished out and I was planning on getting some more...

The second time was better than the first because it lasted longer and I was bolder and more venturesome myself and she finished up moaning and clinging to me and I knew I'd hit the right spot.

This time it was me who put her away from me and I stood up and dusted myself down and then pulled her up and got rid of bits of grass and grit that clung to her dress. She pinned up her bodice and pulled her shawl tight about her so that she could walk back to the ranch without Lola's suspicious glance seeing anything was different.

I rescued the bucket and plunged it deep into the well and cranked the handle for the rope to lift it dripping again. She took it from me with a smile.

'I'll carry it. You go the other way and I'll see you at supper.'

'What about Scufter?'

'What about him?'

'Well, you said he attacked you. He tore your bodice...'

She looked down at herself.

'So he did, but don't worry about Scufter. He's a nuisance but I can handle him.'

'If he tries anything again, let me know, and I'll settle his hash. I can always give him a warning...'

'No! It's not necessary.' She sounded breathless. She smiled appealingly and my attention was riveted on her heaving bosom. In the mood I was in, I was hungry for her and wanted to reach out to her. Gently she moved away and picking up the bucket, lifted her skirt so that her ankle was revealed.

'Lofty,' she went on softly, 'please don't make trouble for Scufter. I can't stand arguments and bad feeling amongst those I'm living with. Promise you'll not say anything?' Her lip trembled and I forgot all my earlier resentments. I was like putty in her hands.

'Kate, I would just give him a hint. I'm not going to shoot his head off or do anything stupid but I don't want him hassling you.'

She dropped the bucket, water spilling over and damping the hem of her skirt.

'Lofty, please, just leave it! I can manage him.'

'But you were crying.'

'Yes, but it wasn't just because of Scufter.'

'Then why...?'

She blinked hard, and now I know with age and experience that women blink hard like that while their brains are whirling around digging up answers. She gave a long drawn-out sigh.

'I was crying because of you!'

'Me?' Hell! Was I startled? I sure was and I got all fluttery inside. 'Me,' I stuttered again, 'why cry over me?'

The eyes fluttered again and now she drew close and put a hand on my shoulder and slowly ran it down to my belt and she played with the buckle.

'Don't you know?' And my Adam's apple shot up and down like an apple in a tub on Hallow'en's night. I coughed and choked.

'I'm not sure. You don't mean...?' She nodded slowly.

'Yes, I was unhappy because you didn't like me.'

'But I thought it was Jed you liked!'

'Oh dear, how blind you men can be! I liked you from the time I laid eyes on you but a girl doesn't like to wear her heart on her sleeve. We've got pride, you know, and it's not very flattering when a man doesn't show he's interested. You were interested, weren't you?' Her lips quivered in a smile.

I gulped and lied. Dammit, you don't tell a female to her face that in the beginning he was suspicious about her, especially when you've had two good romps with her in half an hour!

Then suddenly she was kissing me on the cheek and laughing like crazy and she picked up the bucket and started hurrying towards the house.

Me? I went on walkabout for an hour and inspected the corral fence just so that I could calm down before returning for the evening meal.

I felt guilty as hell. It was going to be hard facing Jed and it would be harder still facing Bonny on the next night. Jesus! That woman sure turned out to be a can of worms!

By the following night I got used to the idea of shagging Kate off. I kidded myself that there was no harm done because she and Jed had no commitment.

I'd been doing some figuring too and Scufter confirmed what I was thinking all unbeknownst. He rode in with old Docherty and grumbled so much about rounding up the strays I knew there was no way he'd ripped that bodice. Kate was lying. But why? The breathtaking idea was that she was lying to get me all sympathetic and have it off in that there scrub, so the bitch must have been telling the truth after all that she wanted me. That was the only conclusion I could think of.

How wrong can a feller get?

Saturday night came and I got rid of my guilt by scrapping with anyone who looked at me a bit cross-eyed. Jed stayed at the ranch and I could imagine what he and Kate were getting up to when the old man went to bed. Now that I'd had a taste of her, I was racked with a kind of jealousy even though Bonny was more loving than usual. Or was it that she sensed the savagery in me? I don't know what turns women on. They seem to like it rough.

I went back to the ranch in a bad mood. I missed Jed's company more than I liked to admit. Scrapping with the locals didn't have the same bite when he wasn't there to watch my back, but I gloried in the bruises and the pain was savagely welcome.

I rode slowly for my ribs ached and I had

a lot of thinking to do. It sure seemed that if I wanted her, I could have Kate, but did I? That was the question and if I did, what had I to offer her? After all, I was living and working at the Bar C just with the promise of what might be mine after old Coggins kicked the bucket.

Apart from my horse and saddle and a small bankroll, I owned nothing. The only way I could be a somebody was to stick with Coggins and Jed and that way I'd never have Kate because I'd never betray Jed. I'd rather ride out than have him knowing about me and her in that scrub.

So I was in sombre mood when I rode into the yard in the moonlight. I dismounted at the corral and unsaddled and opened the gate and slapped my horse on the rump. He galloped off and I humped the saddle to the row of saddlehorses nearby and the pungent smell of steaming horse sweat was in my nose.

Then she was beside me, silent and agitated. I could feel it and see it in her eyes.

She clung to me burying her head in my chest.

'What is it?' I asked and the first thrill of alarm went up and down my spine.

'It's Scufter,' she whispered. 'He got drunk and he said if I didn't go with him, he'd tell Mr Coggins and Jed that I'd slept with you. I don't want that, Lofty! Oh, God, I don't want to hurt them! They've been so good to me. They've given me a home and they trust me! Oh, what shall I do?'

I put her from me.

'Leave him to me. Go into the house and stay there. Where's Jed and the old man?'

'They're not here. Sheriff Newman came and they went into town.'

'Aw hell! Have you been on your lonesome all night? If I'd known...' She smiled with the patience of a saint.

'If you'd known you would have been with me and I shouldn't have had that dreadful scene with Scufter. Oh, Lofty, what shall I do?' Again hysteria threatened to overcome her. I shook her sharply so that her head rocked and I was tempted to slap her cheek but I held back.

'Now you get inside and I'll watch. Go get some sleep. You look washed out.' She went reluctantly inside.

I waited in the shadow of the veranda and twice I had to shake myself awake. The boards creaked and the wind rose and when at last I heard a sound my nerves were jumping, my trigger finger all of a quiver.

Then damn me if the door didn't open and Kate was there in her nightwear and a shawl thrown around her and her hair down and fluffed around her shoulders. I couldn't help but stare for she looked so innocent and years younger.

Then suddenly just as I was going to speak to her, the shadows thickened and moved and she screamed.

'Lofty! He's there! He said he would come for me!' I twisted round and fired from the hip as I'd done during the war, and I went on firing even after I heard the body thrashing on the ground. I was making sure the bastard was dead!

Old Tom Coggins came running. He was in his vest and long johns and his hair awry and I knew that Kate had lied. The old man had been in his bed. A great sickness came over me and I saw her smile triumphantly. It was just a flicker but it had been there and then she was crying hysterically and flinging herself on the body.

I dropped my Colt and turned helplessly to Coggins.

'I didn't know ... I thought it was Scufter....' But Coggins wasn't listening. He was taking aim with that little Derringer he always carried in his sock and he twisted me round with a bullet in the shoulder. I went down and when I came to my senses I was in jail and the doc was cursing while he picked and probed at the bullet lodged there. He passed me a half bottle of rotgut and I gulped it down and sank again into oblivion, and they say I raved for nearly a week.

It was three months before the circuit

judge arrived to hear the case. I thought it would be cut and dried as misadventure but I was tried for murder and Kate Beamish was the main witness against me and told of my jealousy and hatred for Jed Coggins and that I was ready and willing to bite the hand of the man that fed me.

Kate married old Coggins while I waited for the judge. It made quite a stir but as the old biddies said, old Coggins needed an heir for all that land and Lofty Williams wouldn't get a sniff of it, and that poor innocent creature needed looking after, and who better to do it than poor Jed Coggins's pa?

It only took a half-day for the jury to come up with a guilty verdict. After all, it was obvious. Lofty Williams put paid to Jed Coggins so that he could marry Kate Beamish and cash in on his friendship with old Coggins. But he'd come unstuck and no one in his right mind would believe Lofty's story, after Kate fluttered her eyelashes and told her story. And so the jury argued it and came up with their answers and none of 'em realized they were being manipulated....

So despite Bonny Bluefeathers and all Charlie's girls and the testimonies of our drinking buddies as to Jed's and my closeness, I was bundled back into jail with the word guilty ringing in my ears and the memory of Kate clinging to old Coggins and he still murderously angry fit to kill.

It was that night Bonny surpassed herself and I had to listen to the deputy's grunts and groans as they frolicked during my last supposed night on this earth.

But before morning I was long gone. Bonny, grinning and swaying happily having matched drink for drink with the deputy waved his bunch of keys in the air when at last he collapsed.

'Come on, don't muck about,' I said roughly for I hadn't liked the way she'd evidently enjoyed herself.

She opened the grille smiling widely, and then screwed her eyes up and puckered her lips expecting a hug and a kiss.

I was an ungrateful bastard and I was sore

at her because she moaned louder with him than she ever had with me.

I left her without a word.

Bonny had a good store of cuss words and when she was het up she could frazzle the air at a dozen paces.

And oh boy! How she frazzled the air that night!

## THREE

I made a big mistake when I left Bonny so hurriedly. But I could feel the noose tightening about my neck and it was turning my guts to water. I should have stopped and given her a little time and it would have saved me grief later on.

But I didn't. She'd no sooner told me that Shaggy Cotton was behind the livery stable with my horse saddled and ready to go than I was off with her yelling blue murder after me.

It had been a stroke of genius on Bonny's part to get Shaggy in on the escape. No one would believe that he would ever lift a finger to help me after all the batterings he'd taken over the years.

But folk would have been wrong. Me and Jed and Shaggy Cotton and Dicky Jones understood each other. We all enjoyed those Saturday-night scraps and now those two guys would have to find new sparring partners to cuss and beat up.

We grinned at each other behind the barn and then shook hands. I was going to miss that broken nose, those cross eyes and the gap-toothed grin more than I ever thought possible.

'Good luck, pard. Me and Dicky said all along you never meant to kill Jed. You had a tough break, feller.'

I nodded, too cut up to say much for that noose sat uneasily on me and I wanted to be away. Then I remembered Bonny.

'You'll watch out for Bonny?' I mumbled.

'Yeh, she's a good kid. She's gonna miss you, Lofty.'

Again I nodded. I was realizing just how much I cared for the dumpy round-faced halfbreed Bonny Bluefeathers. I could see her plump rather flat face framed by two thick plaits of hair and how she liked me to tug them during our romps... Hell! I was missing those romps. It seemed an age since we'd cuddled up together. Since being banged up I hadn't even felt the urge, what with my wound and everything.

I was even up to thinking my tackle wasn't any good any more! I wished I'd had time to try it out on Bonny to put me to rights.

I forked my horse and looked down at Shaggy.

'Well, you son of a gun, this is it. Sorry I broke your nose, pal. It wasn't deliberate.'

'Sure.' He nodded tight-lipped. 'I never was a good-looker, anyway ... and that cracked shoulder of yours…' he grinned wickedly, 'I was aiming at your head!'

'So we're quits!' I reached down holding out my hand. He gripped it tight. There was no more to be said.

Then I broke the hold and gripped my horse's belly with my knees and felt his muscles tighten for that first leap forward and giving a piercing rebel yell I thundered into the night.

The next few weeks were belly-tightening.

I was like an animal. There was a posse one day behind me. I travelled at night and hunted by night and holed up during the day. I shunned the trails and kept well away from white men and towns. I thirsted for some real liquor but fought the urge to go find it.

Bonny had filled a gunny sack with possibles and so what with them and a few jackrabbits and once a young buck, I managed to merge into the wilderness.

It was a hard life and yet I not only survived but actually put weight on my bony body. I grew to love the great silences, the sough of the wind in the tall pines and the clean mountain air unpolluted by cows.

It was a time of discovery about myself. I had time to grieve properly for Jed whereas before in jail, I was concentrating all my thoughts on my own survival. I lived that moment over and over again when I shot him. It came night after night to haunt me until at last I had had enough and I began to fight back and think of the events that led up to it, and each time I came back to Kate and each time I realized that she had deliberately planned to get rid of the two of us and leave her free to target the old man.

I remembered the three times he came to visit me in jail. There was no affection from the past. Just accusation. I had killed his son and so I was his enemy.

That hurt for I had come to genuinely like the often stubborn old man. He was like another father to me and I respected his rather narrow ways. Indeed, I held him in affection. So when he left for the last time, saying he would not come again for reasons he would not say, I was cut to the heart. Of course after his marriage to Kate, I realized who was putting words into his mouth.

So all that was behind me and I had time to ponder on my own life and what I should do with it.

It all boiled up to what I should do about Kate. Each time I thought of her and her devilish allure, I was obsessed by the notion she should pay for Jed's death and for the ruin of my life.

Yet I could not go back openly to face her and bring about her retribution.

One night I had a dream. I awakened suddenly and sat up with my eyes wide open staring straight ahead. The answer to it all was plain. Why hadn't I thought of it sooner?

I rekindled the fire and brewed up the remains of last night's coffee and sat drinking and staring into the flames and my mind went on from that first revealing dream. I should make my aim Chicago, and work in the stockyards and then in the great abbatoirs. I should tackle Kate Beamish Coggins from Chicago...

I already knew the name Coggins was well known in Chicago for hadn't Jed and me sent off regular consignments of beef to the meat factories there?

It was going to take guts and hard work and a dedicated obsession to stand the life in the meatyards. It was going to be hell but worth it.

I was right: it was hell.

It took two years, and a balding thatch of grey hair to get to be foreman in the Dufton Meat Packing Corporation, and another four years of dedicated hardship to get out of the blood and stink of the abbatoirs to set up my own business of supplying cheap second-class meat for the Chinese coolies working for the big railway construction agencies.

But in those years there had been the isolated satisfactions of putting various spokes into the Coggins' wheels.

There had been the rumours of ticks in the herds and the price in the Chicago yards had dropped alarmingly. It had been well worth paying for a few infested animals to be infiltrated amongst the Coggins beef!

The Coggins cheque for that year must have been halved.

Then there had been the scare of foot and mouth disease, and then the outbreak of worms...

It had all cost the Coggins Bar C a hell of an amount of hard cash.

It had been more years than I cared to

remember to think back to those eventful and gruelling years. The woman I never forgot: she was there in my mind continuously.

Even all the long years I was eventually married to Bonny, she never realized that Kate lay between us, mocking, unsilent and triumphant.

I came back to the present with a start. The man before me was touching my arm.

'Sir...'

I blinked. It was like being wrenched through a time warp and it hurt. I suppose I looked like a doddering old man who'd nodded off.

I straightened my shoulders and shuffled my legs in the club chair to gain a little time to pull myself together.

'Yes ... yes,' I said testily. It always paid to be brusque. I was beginning to appreciate old man Coggins's stubbornness. 'I'm not sleeping, only closing my eyes while I consider your suggestion.'

The man before me smiled with a

crookedness that was somehow familiar. He was tall and around forty and muscular. He looked as if he'd spent his whole life in the saddle, as indeed he had. This was the son of old Tom Coggins and his wife Kate.

I'd never imagined that over the years I'd sit in the same room as Kate's son and listen to him expound on an idea of amalgamating the Coggins Bar C Cattle Company with that of the N S Williams Wholesale Meat Corporation.

'Well? How does it grab you, Mr Williams?'

Kate's eyes regarded me with some curiosity. I could feel it. It wasn't personal, more the regard of a man for a legend, to prove to himself if the great Norman S Williams was the Midas man he was cracked up to be.

'Not so fast, young feller. I'd want to know more about your finances and your background than I do now! I know I'm old but I'm not an old fool.'

'But I thought you were aware of the Coggins standing! We've had dealings on and off for years. Why, ever since my father died, we've had good relations!'

'That's all very well, son, but dealing with is very different to throwing in with anyone. How do I know you're not on your uppers? There's been some bad drought years and there's been years when you never sent your herds to Chicago.'

'But there were good reasons. We had it tough for many years but we survived. We concentrated on breeding up new stocks. We spent money on expensive Mexican bulls immune to disease and ticks...'

I nodded, hard put not to laugh. I'd contributed to some of the Coggins' bad luck. I hope Kate Beamish Coggins had to do her own housework and wear coarse underwear next to that satin smooth skin...

'Yeh, well times were hard for all of us,' I commented and remembered the time I slipped back into Abilene and brought back Bonny Bluefeathers and married her in the small chapel in Chicago.

But it had been the wrong thing to do. By

then I was what she would call rich, and I would call affluent. By that I meant that I had a nice white-painted house set back in a good-sized yard and I could afford Bonny a servant and a coachman and her own natty runabout so she could air it amongst the snooty town biddies.

She stood it for nearly five years and then it broke her heart and she lost interest in me and life. She regarded herself as a failure for we had no family and so she lost her comeliness and her face took on a gaunt yearning which I could never understand, and so she slipped away one evening just before Thanksgiving.

I missed Bonny Bluefeathers then more than I did when I rode away and left her without a thank you all those years before.

It was hard to face. I killed her all unknowingly. I'd taken her from her own environment and she'd sickened with that mystery thing called homesickness. Poor Bonny Bluefeathers ... it should never have happened, but I was a vigorous man in those days intent on dragging myself up from the blood and muck of the abbatoirs and couldn't see what was under my nose...

Again, those years had brought back memories as this burly man spoke of their hard years.

'I must examine your books. I'll have one of my clerks come out to your ranch.'

'But that will take weeks!'

'Why should it? A couple of days on the train. Three days at the outside to go through your holdings and a couple of days back and so one week should see it through.'

'But it can't wait. Mr Williams, I want a decision today!'

I suddenly knew that this was the moment I'd been waiting for all these years. I had Kate Beamish Coggins in the hollow of my hand.

'You're broke, aren't you?'

For a moment he was rigidly still. He flushed and I saw his Adam's apple move up and down like one of these newfangled clacks and then he nodded.

'Yes.'

I experienced a great rush of pleasure. It caused a flush of blood to course through me. I felt renewed, triumphant and actually light-headed.

'What about your family ... your mother...?'

'She knows but my wife doesn't. Amy's not interested in the running of the ranch. She's interested in the kids and the welfare of our hands. We've got married cowhands and she takes her responsibilities rather more than my mother should.'

'Your mother ran the Bar C after your father died, I understand?'

Young Tom Coggins flushed.

'Yeh, there was a time when I left home through my mother's stubbornness. She is a very strong-willed lady.'

'I can imagine. She saw the ranch through some very bad years what with the drought and all.'

'We don't see eye to eye now actually. She strongly disapproves of my coming to you.'

'Oh? And why is that?'

Surely Kate wasn't astute enough to know that Norman S Williams was the gangly Lofty? Tom Coggins shrugged heavy shoulders. He didn't look anything like poor old Jed being taller, wider and darker. He didn't look like Kate either except for his eyes which were the same peculiar blue ... Irish eyes, reminding one of blue pools after rain...

'Ma always had a thing about bankers. Always made out they robbed folk blind. She thinks anyone who's made money is automatically some kind of chiseller. She thinks if we merge with another company then that company will take advantage and cook the books somehow.'

'And you don't think I should do that?'

'No. We should both engage honest clerks to represent our own interests. I think if we cut out the middle man and raise our own beef and ship it direct to our own meat plant, we could save money...'

'And you could take advantage of the existing accounts and contracts and raise your beef according to what is required every given year?'

'Exactly, Mr Williams, you've got it in one. I shouldn't have to compete against all the other cattle barons. We'd be keeping it in the family, so to speak.'

'You're shrewd, boy. You certainly take after your old man. I'll think on it. Come back tomorrow.'

He moved well and I was more impressed than I admitted to myself. I liked the boy. It was a pity he had Kate for a mother. Somehow I was expecting him to take on her deviousness and I was on the lookout for the first hint of double-cross.

He turned at the door, hat in hand.

'Thank you for listening, Mr Williams. Now I must go and convince my mother.'

'She's here in town with you?'

'Yes. She wouldn't hear tell of me coming to Chicago alone. Said she was coming for Amy's sake, to keep me out of woman trouble, but I know different. She still thinks I'm wet behind the ears!'

I laughed. I could imagine Kate manipulating her boy and watching him grow to manhood and not conceding that he could look after his own affairs. I wondered how he'd ever come to marry or had she engineered that too? The thought made me curious.

'What about your wife? Is she here too?'

'No. She expects a baby in two months and the doctor did not advise the travel. She's rather delicate and we had trouble with the other births.'

'How many children have you, Tom?'

'Four when this one arrives, two boys and a girl and Amy hopes for another girl. I shouldn't mind another boy.'

He grinned suddenly and the years dropped off him and he reminded me of how Jed and I had been.

It was then I made up my mind, but I wasn't going to tell him. He could come hat in hand tomorrow and do a bit more begging. So I said instead, 'Tell your ma she can come and visit me here at the Cattleman's

Club. I come in most days and stay until evening. She can have tea like a lady. She can come whenever she likes.'

'I'll tell her, Mr Williams. I think she'll be right pleased to get your invite. She likes a bit of social life. She don't get none back home in Abilene. She don't go down with the townsfolk for some reason. Never mixes with the ladies of the town or goes to church meetings. A strange woman, my ma.'

I nodded. I couldn't agree with him more but I couldn't voice what I thought of her to this open-faced man who was nothing like the woman I'd hated nearly all my life.

Later that day a messenger brought a well-scripted note to say that Mrs Kate Coggins would call on the following day at precisely four o'clock to take tea.

I estimated that Tom Coggins's business would be over before his mother called and I was right. Tom called at eleven o'clock and at noon we were shaking hands. We had a deal. He was overwhelmingly grateful and my first cynical reaction changed to a surprising warmth. Surprising because it was unlooked for.

There was no getting away from the fact I liked this man and it was something I'd shied away from all my life since the day I killed Jed.

To me, emotion was dangerous. I had even kept poor Bonny at a distance and she never understood it. On reflection perhaps that was partly why she could never settle in Chicago. Maybe I should take more blame for Bonny's death than I ever had.

These whirling notions going on inside my head were like wispy threads. It was all tumbling around and out, now that I had started the process of remembering.

I was coming to despise myself and I didn't know why.

Maybe it was the poison of revenge that was seeping through every pore of my body. I think I was beginning to stink with it.

But I couldn't change the thinking of forty years. I still hated Kate Beamish's guts and always would.

I gave Tom instructions as to what to do next and a written letter for my bank explaining the agreement and that Mr Dukes was to visit me and draw up the legal papers.

I still experienced the thrill of demanding and getting servile service from the financial fraternity. I always got that thrill up my spine that denoted power. I felt myself straighten and stretch two inches taller. It was a good feeling.

I lunched as I usually did, for the club was famed for good meals and I hated being alone in my fine house just off Main Street. It wasn't a home any more since Bonny died. It was just a museum of fine furniture and pictures and womanly knicknacks that hurt me when I happened to notice them, which wasn't often: I purposely didn't look.

So I suppose I didn't know when my slatternly housekeeper shortchanged me and didn't dust and clean as she should, or report breakages. Now and again I missed something, but old Moll had been with me ever since Bonny died and I wasn't going to upset her by implying she'd nicked something or broke it. Let sleeping dogs lie, I have always maintained and as long as she keeps my clothes clean and my bed, I couldn't care less.

However uneasy thoughts of the past were coming thick and fast and now a nasty little thought was intruding. Had I worked all these years just to become a lonely old man eaten up with a canker of revenge? Hell! I'd never looked at it that way before.

What the hell was happening to me?

Why was my mind and life being tipped arse over end?

I slept uneasily after my lunch and I think I dreamed because I woke up confused and in a black sweat. I could hear a quiet knocking on the smoking-room door. It was usually empty at this time of day except for myself, and the porter's head came round the door.

'Excuse me, Mr Williams, sir, but there's a lady to see you. She says she's expected.'

I pulled out my gold turnip watch and

looked at it. Bless me, it was four o'clock and I'd wanted at least an hour to prepare myself for her visit and I could not blame anyone but myself for sleeping too soundly.

'Send her in,' and I sounded gruff even to myself.

My heart beat fast as I waited for her. How would she look now after all these years and would she recognize me? That was the big question.

I tensed as I heard her footsteps beyond the door and then she was moving towards me, a rather bent old lady with smooth white hair and leaning on a silver-topped cane.

I struggled to my feet, suddenly feeling giddy, and went to meet her.

'You're very welcome, Mrs Coggins. Come, sit down and I'll ring the bell for tea. It is all arranged.'

She sank gracefully into the chair opposite the wide fireplace. It was of scarlet velvet and framed her nicely. She was wearing black and looked affluent and very very dignified. I wondered whether this was all part of a show to impress me. I noted the cameo brooch at her neck and the diamond drops in her ears. This didn't look like a woman who was on the breadline.

'I am very pleased to meet you, Mr Williams,' she breathed softly and fidgeted with her purse.

'And I'm very pleased to have you here,' I said, very gallant, though I wasn't used to being polite to the ladies. I'd given up a certain kind of woman years ago when the juices dried up and as for the respectable town wives, I steered clear. Those kind could be trouble if you even raised an eyebrow at them.

We were both awkward and no doubt thinking the same things for after the tea table came, she said with a rush, 'No doubt my son told you I disapproved of him coming to you?'

'Yes, but I still can't understand why.'

'Because we Cogginses have been free all our lives and beholden to no man and I think my son should work and strive as we did in the old days. It was never easy...'

'But you married a wealthy man, Mrs Coggins.'

She sat up very straight, shoulders thrown back and I saw something of the old Kate, the tempestuous, proud, overbearing Kate who must have her own way.

'How do you know that? We've never met before, have we?'

I breathed a sigh of relief and yet it was of disappointment too. I wanted to see her shock when she recognized me, if she ever did. If she didn't, then I should have to inflict the sword thrust myself. Looking at her now, I wasn't very sure that I could do so. She wasn't the raven-haired Irish girl who'd plotted and planned any more. She was a genteel old lady with lots of dignity and charm. I shrugged.

'Tom Coggins was well known and when he married again the whole world knew it. The marriage was news, you know. There were those who questioned his good sense for taking a young wife.' I couldn't help my voice grating.

The soft wrinkled skin flushed; the slightly faded blue eyes sparked.

'I was a good wife and there were reasons why I should wed, which are none of your business. Anyway, it was all a long time ago and for years I ran the Bar C and I ran it well.'

'There's no doubt about that. I must hand it to you, Mrs Coggins, you know your cows!'

'And I still do as I keep telling my son! I still have the last say in what goes on at the ranch. My husband left me the ranch wholly and fully and it's legal. My son lives with me at my invitation only and if he doesn't like it, then he knows what to do!'

'Are you as hard as you make out, Mrs Coggins?'

She thinned her lips and now I could see the hardness of her. Her backbone came up straight and proud and they were the only signs she gave to my question, but fiddled at the tea table with the milk and sugar.

'Tea with milk and sugar?' she asked in a tight voice.

'Just sugar. These days I like my tea sweet if I'm forced to drink it.'

Her lips twitched.

'I am not too much of a lady, Mr Williams, that I should be shocked if you preferred something stronger at this time.'

I grunted.

'Tea will do quite nicely seeing's I'm paying for it,' I said, engrossed in her remark about being no lady. If she knew the half of it! I could take the starch out of her any time I wished!

It gave me a lot of pleasure to sit there watching her, having had carnal knowledge of her, and she, like a juicy black fly not yet struggling in my web...

Then she raised her fine eyes to mine.

'Do you mind telling me what arrangements you have made with my son?'

'Yes, I mind. This is man's business and I'm not prepared to talk to you. I'm old-fashioned, ma'am, and I believe that women should keep their place.'

'Even though I have been an independent woman for years?'

I bowed my head. I was damned if I was going to talk about Tom's business. After all, he had come to me, not the other way round. Mind you, being fair, I must admit to manoeuvring them into the position they are today by backdoor methods and a bit of good old-fashioned blackmail of my financial associates. It's bloody surprising what can be done in the background. I was and am a good puppeteer.

I watched her anger vie with caution. She knew she was in no position to anger me. I only wish I was aware of Coggins's true financial position. Not that it mattered in the final outcome. I must make a mental note to put Saltash, my private hound on the subject of Kate Beamish Coggins's private affairs. She could well be holding out on her son. That lady could well stoop low enough to twist her only child.

At last she could contain herself no longer.

'Mr Williams, I have never been so insulted in my life! I have conducted my own business in the stockyards, bought and sold my cows to my own advantage...'

'So why does your son come to me?' I slipped in with rapier thrust. She flushed.

'I'm not responsible for weather conditions and drought. We had some bad years and then we were unfortunate in getting infestations of ticks and worms through no fault of our own. We have had bad luck...'

'Excuses ... excuses.... You had the same chances as other ranchers. You should have let your son take over. He would have been less emotional and more practical!' I watched with secret pleasure as I goaded her.

At last she stood upright with a jerk that rocked the flimsy tea table.

'I think it is time to leave,' she said with awful majesty designed to overawe me but didn't impress me one iota. I could only see her as a calculating ruthless female who destroyed the lives of two young men and persuaded a rich broken-hearted old man to marry her. Out of that marriage had come one good thing, a child, a half-brother for Jed whom he never knew.

There was only one thing I hadn't calculated on and that was that I might find myself liking the young man. I suppose it was because old Tom Coggins was his father and I had had some affection for the old man.

'Yeh, you might say that, ma'am. I don't think we have much to talk about at the moment. You ask Tom about our arrangements and you can also tell him I have changed my mind on his suggestion.'

'And what might that be?'

I savoured the moment. I smiled and I watched her brace herself. She was a very astute woman.

'Tell him that you have changed my mind and when I've got all my outstanding affairs in order, I'll come and visit the Bar C Ranch for a time.'

Her face registered alarm and puzzlement

and shock.

'I don't understand. Are you taking over the Bar C?' Fury bloated her eyes with blood.

'No, ma'am. Just making sure you have the stock your son guarantees, and that it's in prime condition. At my time of life I find I don't have God's own trust in folk like I did!'

'I think you are a rude, offensive man, Mr Williams!'

'You do? Well, maybe that's a good thing. I'm sure not a good man to make an enemy of, ma'am, which you might find out!'

'Mr Williams, I don't know what this is all about, this talk of enemies and not trusting. I'm sure my son has told you all the truth, as he sees it. I'm afraid we rather got off on the wrong foot.' She held out a hand. 'Can we not forget what has been said and start again? I'm sorry I was rude. I'm not used to such cavalier treatment.'

'No, I don't imagine you are. Most men will fall over themselves to deal with you. I expect you've got the best of many deals because you're a woman!'

She was taken aback and her hand which I ignored dropped to her side.

'Mr Williams, just who are you? And what do you really want?'

I paused to savour the situation a little longer.

'You're a very discerning woman, Mrs Coggins. Yes, I must admit there is something of yours I want, but as for who I am, I've yet to make up my mind about myself.'

'I really don't follow you, Mr Williams.'

'Good. Then we'll leave it at that then?'

## FOUR

It had been a long sooty journey and I was glad when it was over. Truth to tell, I was feeling my age for the first time, or was it that now that my years of revenge were nearly over? I was beginning to wonder whether the enjoyment had been in the imagining of it. Now that I knew Kate and saw her once more in the flesh and how old and frail she looked, I was beginning to have second thoughts.

There was also Tom, and Kate for all her evil, was his ma. Not that he seemed too fond of her. Indeed on the few occasions we were all together, before they entrained for Abilene, they did not seem to agree on anything.

I remembered back to the day when Saltash came sneaking into my room at the club, hat twisting in hand and looking like a bright-eyed crow with his long pointed nose and black bankteller's garb. He had a habit too, of cocking his head on one side as he talked. He was really a nasty little piece of work but essential if I was to keep one step ahead of my associates and enemies.

The meat-packing trade and the many contracts for hotels and road-gangs took some organizing and I had to sniff out tenders somehow, and Saltash did the sniffing for me.

He hadn't surprised me when he told me about the Coggins set-up.

'Yes, yes, I already know she owns the ranch and that he and she own the stock,' I had exclaimed testily when he had come to me with that sly look on his face that meant news.

'But there's more than that, Mr Williams,' and he coughed into his hand. I knew the gesture. I sighed.

'Very well, Saltash, the usual rates, but get on with it!'

He gave his customary smirk and then said softly, 'She has connections going back many years and from a source which I might add was expensive to myself, I found someone who knew her many years ago in San Francisco.'

I sat up with a jerk. This was news indeed!

'And when would that be?'

'Oh, my informant thinks about forty-five years since she put five thousand dollars into what might be called a cathouse, begging your pardon, sir, but you did request a summary of the lady's activities and any monies thereof.'

'True, Saltash. I'm not complaining. You mean she's been collecting her dividends ever since?'

'Yes, sir. Made out to a firm of lawyers in San Francisco and banked in the name of Kate Beamish. There are also other monies accruing from a milliner's shop, a grocery and liquor store, a saloon and a boarding-house, all managed separately so that none interferes with the rest.'

I took a deep breath. So the bitch let that boy worry his guts out about making that damned ranch pay while she piled up the golden mountain. I wondered if she expected to take it with her when she cocked her toes!

So now I looked at her with this new knowledge in me. She was with Tom and his wife and their children who had honoured me by coming to meet the train.

I stepped down gingerly for my old legs were stiff with sitting. The children looked at me with wonder and a great rush of feeling overcame me as I looked as their innocent eyes. They were the ones I was hurting with my underhand dealings to get the ranch into my clutches.

Tom introduced his wife after I had acknowledged Kate's stiff greeting. I concluded privately that she wasn't going to allow anything to be said between us all that she could not listen in to.

I liked Amy. She was small and neat with fair hair and pretty blue eyes and a motherly manner. She had just got out of bed from giving birth to her fourth child, a girl whom she was calling Sophie. She looked a little pale and apprehensive of her ma-in-law, otherwise she was happy to be with Tom.

I thought she was the ideal helpmate for him and that he was a lucky man.

Kate didn't seem to think so for she was highhanded with the girl on the ride home to the ranch. Tom did not hear the exchange for he was riding a magnificent chestnut gelding which made me feel like forking a horse again for old time's sake.

I saw Amy flush and felt sorry for her. I decided to intervene.

'The gal's fine, Mrs Coggins. I'm sure we all understand children should be seen and not heard, but meeting the train is exciting in itself. What's your name, child?'

Amy rushed in before the shy child could find her tongue.

'This is Annie, and I'm sure she didn't really fidget on purpose. They're good-mannered children as a rule and so is the baby. We've called her Sophie...'

'You've already told him that, Amy. Do be quiet. I'm sure Mr Williams isn't interested in your stories about the children. I told you to leave them at home but you would insist that they come too. They take up so much room in the wagon, you know. One cannot stretch one's legs.'

'We'll manage, ma'am. It would have been a shame to deprive them of a treat.'

Amy looked at me with a grateful smile and quietly pressed my hand and I smiled back. We shared a secret.

Kate snorted and glared at Amy who cowered a little and seemed to grow smaller.

I was beginning to think it was time Kate got a part of her comeuppance.

I wasn't prepared for the torrent of feeling that overwhelmed me when we first came in sight of the ranch. I saw at a glance it had been added to, no doubt when she had first married old Tom. Indeed, I remembered it as an unpainted square box of a place with a long, low, deep veranda.

Now there were signs of long-gone white

paint grown shabby over the years and an extra long extension to add further rooms to what had been a tightly knit bachelor domain.

She had made sure Tom had given her a home with style. I could see that in its heyday it would have been a wonderful proud place in which to live.

The outside buildings and the bunkhouse were very much the same as before except for a new barn, at least it had been new. Now it looked weatherbeaten and uncared for. The corral fences too needed renewing and there was an air of hopelessness about the whole place.

It should have pleased me, but it didn't. I felt ashamed that I should have plotted for the ruin of this place that I had regarded as my home.

As my eyes moved slowly past the vista of buildings and corrals, I could hear old Tom's voice once again: 'Aye, boys, look at it well. It's all yours to share equally so the harder you work, the more hours you put in, the more you're working for yourselves! It's all yours, boys. It's your heritage; yours, Jed, and yours, Lofty, for it's big enough for both of you. You've got an empire to control when the time comes!'

I'd heard him say that, times without number and now his words were ringing in my ears.

I looked my fill and then I looked at Kate and something surely in my eyes made her turn away. I struggled with myself for I was trembling with reaction.

'So this is the famous Bar C, home of the legendary Tom Coggins, who dominated the cattle trails forty years ago!'

Young Tom, who had ridden up when the wagon stopped, heard my words. He laughed.

'That was all in another time, before I was born. There's been many ups and downs since those days. But maybe the Bar C will rise again and become as famous as it was in those days.'

'I sincerely hope so,' I growled, 'or I

shouldn't be here!'

There were several cowhands lounging around when we finally drew up in front of the ranchhouse. I frowned. I didn't like paid hands wasting time and money, especially here where so many jobs needed doing. I resolved to give them a blast or two when I got my second wind.

I had a feeling the hands took advantage of two bosses and one of 'em a woman. It was becoming my considered opinion that Tom Coggins was too nice and he hadn't a rough enough tongue or his ma's backbone to control either her or his men properly. I was going to make some changes, by damn!

Tom helped his ma down from the wagon and I clambered down close behind and then helped Amy to alight. She was like a feather, dainty and yet womanly and nicely curved. I could understand Tom's feeling for her. If I'd been thirty years younger I would have taken her myself.

She looked up breathlessly and laughed then blushed as I steadied her and the pink bloom brought her to life. She would be a different little lady when her mother-in-law was gone...

That phrase hit me. What was I going to do about that old woman? There she was, a slender, slightly bent figure in black, supervising the handling of my boxes and portmanteaus and already she must have guessed by the amount of luggage that I was planning for a longtime stay. The black widow...

She must have sensed my eyes on her for she turned and looked at me and then at Amy.

'Don't stand making sheep's eyes at Mr Williams, Amy! Take him inside and for once play the hostess if it's possible!'

Again, Amy flushed and swallowed and I took her arm and quietly led her up the veranda steps to the welcome shade and then into a cool hall with a brightly polished wooden floor that smelled of beeswax and womanly hard work.

I sensed the welcome in the house, the bunch of flowers in the vase, the waiting jug of iced beer and I also was aware of something else, a touch of evil...

I nodded at the flowers. 'Your idea? How did you know I liked flowers?'

Amy laughed up at me ... she laughed easily when not cowed.

'I didn't. I just thought they would be nice. They're so beautiful I was sure they would give you pleasure. I put another bunch in your room. I hope you don't mind?'

'Mind? Of course not. It's been a long time since anyone pampered me.'

'Then let me pour you a beer and then I shall take you upstairs. Sam and the boys will see to your luggage and Mother-in-law has it all in hand.'

I drank beer and watched a bald-headed man and a youth struggle up the uncarpeted stairs with my portmanteau. The bald-headed man looked none too happy. Two more men came in with my bags and then I was being ushered into a long, low, cool room that was evidently the main living-room. It was untidy and homely, with a small pile of baby garments laid about as if just been stitched and there were a couple of ledgers as if Tom had been studying them prior to coming to the station.

There were also a number of neatly piled toys, a wooden doll, some lead soldiers and a replica railway engine complete with carriages and trucks. There was also the smell of a baby who'd been sick...

Amy looked uncomfortable as she showed me around, apologizing for the untidiness and also the smell. It didn't worry me and I told her so but before we could remove ourselves, Kate came in and made herself unpleasant about 'babies should be seen at intervals and then kept quietly and discreetly in the kitchen quarters'.

At this, Amy nearly fired up. I wondered what it would take for Amy to really forget herself and give as good as she got.

I shut Kate up by saying briefly, 'That's a load of bollocks, ma'am. I use that term because perhaps it's a term you know best since you're an expert on cows, and talking of cows...' I looked her up and down and made it plain that I was comparing her to a cow. She pinched her mouth together so that it looked like a duck's arse, all the little wrinkles folding in to themselves and I laughed at her discomfiture. I was a bit sorry that Amy was there to witness it and that the girl would suffer privately.

I couldn't fathom why Kate didn't like Amy or the children. Dammit, any mother would like a daughter-in-law like Amy who wouldn't say boo to a goose and would be proud of her grandchildren. It was weird.

Over a couple of days I found the boys, George and Harry, kept out of her way while Annie hid behind her mother's skirts especially when their grandmother was about.

I also became acquainted with the baby's wet-nurse, a young Indian girl who had lost her baby and had been abandoned by her tribe. She reminded me of Bonny Blue-feathers when I first saw her all those years ago.

The girl, Water-That-Ripples-Over-Stones, and whom Amy called, Ripple, was sitting at the cookhouse door breast-feeding the bundle that was the baby. She looked very much like Bonny would have done if she'd ever been blessed with a child.

I warmed to her for that reason alone. She looked up at me as I stopped to speak and look at the little fair head and the greedy mouth sucking away at the full breast. The sight touched me deeply.

'And how is little Sophie today?'

The girl smiled and nodded and held the baby up proudly.

'She take much milk. She grow like weed. Very good. No cry,' and she beamed as if indeed she was her own.

I leaned on my stick and settled myself to spend a few minutes finding out about this squaw whom Kate did not approve of having around the ranch.

We talked, and soon I had the picture of a girl who'd forsaken her wandering tribe for the settled life with a white man, and when that white man got drunk in a saloon and shot in a drunken brawl she had been kicked out of her cowboy's shack and told to leave the territory although she was heavily pregnant at the time.

She did not grieve over the man but over losing her permanent home. She had wandered for weeks living on herbs and roots that she recognized from her time with the tribe. Her baby had been born without aid and was weakly from the start. It died and she would have died herself if she hadn't been found by one of the Bar C cowhands looking for strays.

It had been at the time of Amy's lying-in and she, having little or no milk, welcomed the Indian woman who had known at once what was required of her. Calmly she had taken the crying baby and put her to her breast, and she had taken charge of her ever since, much to Kate's snobbish horror, even though Tom patiently pointed out that the baby might have died without Ripple's help.

So there was another loyal person for Amy

and somehow I knew she needed all those around her who were loyal to her.

One day after the evening meal when we were all stretched out a little sleepy after good food and several mugs of home-made beer, Kate made us all extremely alert when she said with some sour satisfaction, 'It's time you two men shaved. I think it is disgusting that you should both look like a couple of cowhands. You're supposed to be gentlemen! I find it very distasteful that Amy and I should sit here and watch you two snore like two bristly pigs!'

Tom and I looked at each other. His beard was black and aggressively bristly, mine was thin and grey and straggly. I ran my hands through my chin whiskers. Maybe the woman had a point. It was a sloppy way to get into I had to agree. We both looked at Amy for the final verdict and she, poor dear, looked embarrassed.

'Well? What do you think, Amy?'

She bit her lip. 'I'm sure I don't mind.'

I could hear Kate snort in the background. 'Trust that little ninny not to have a mind of her own!'

I saw the struggle in Amy, and then, 'Look, I try not to criticize. I love Tom, no matter what he looks like and surely it is up to him how he looks and dresses? We do not criticize you, Mother-in-law, indeed we should not dare! And as for Mr Williams here, he is our guest and should do as he likes!'

With that long speech, she cowered down again as if the spurt of rebellion had drained her once again. She needed to for Kate's eyes spat bullets and Amy would suffer later in private.

'I still think you both look like drifters and men of no consequence. I shall be ashamed of you both when you visit Abilene.'

'So that's it, is it?' Tom said gruffly. 'You're worried about what the neighbours think? That the Cogginses are on the downward path. Has-beens. Wash-outs!'

Kate stiffened herself.

'And why not? I've got pride and I don't

want anyone from this ranch adding to rumours that I know abound. And that means you, Mr Williams, as you are now bound to our fortunes for good or ill.'

'Well said, Mrs Coggins, ma'am. I quite see your logic. I shall present you with a clean shaven face in the morning. Will that satisfy you?'

She smiled in triumph and shot a darkling glance at both her son and Amy. No doubt, Tom would appear on the morrow, duly shaved and minus his beard.

The next morning when I wielded the cut-throat and washed away the lather I fleetingly wondered whether Kate should recognize me. But the face that looked back at me from the mirror was so very different to that of all those years ago. There was no sign of the gangly Lofty. There was just this bald-headed oldster with tufts of nearly white hair, with fuller grooved cheeks and a stubborn look to his mouth. The nose protruded as of old, but a woman wouldn't remember in forty years...

So I wasn't prepared for her reaction when I went looking for breakfast in the cookhouse and found a clean-shaven Tom sitting eating steak and biscuits and Kate fussing at the stove.

She turned and gave me one look, turned a little pale and then gave a high laugh.

'Goodness me! You look like a person I knew a long, long time ago. I thought for a moment you were he!'

'You looked as if the devil was after you. Have you a naughty skeleton in your cupboard, Mrs Coggins?'

For a moment the question rattled her and then she recovered.

'Don't be foolish, it doesn't become you, Mr Williams. Sit down and I'll dish up.' She turned her back on me and for a few moments busied herself at the stove. She was flushed when she slammed down my plate of steak and the hot biscuits.

She was rattled all right and I grinned to myself. I had a feeling Kate Beamish was finding that she was walking on broken egg-shells. I compared her look now with that of the day she came to tea at my club and I felt a great satisfaction that now she looked worn and unrested.

Soon, she would be like a black female cougar, cornered, spitting, claws rending anyone within reach. I was the hunter. Then she would be really dangerous.

But when Tom and I were preparing to ride out and inspect the stock, she insisted on coming along. She smiled sweetly and said she needed the exercise and wanted to get away from a household full of children and diapers.

She rode well. She forked her horse like a man in an old black habit and a wide black stetson jammed down over her hair. A touch of white at her chin was the only relief. She was still a handsome woman and she knew it.

We took some chuck and lunched far out on the range. We'd passed several herds of beef. I noted their condition and that of the pasture and did some rough calculations in my head as to numbers and was surprised and pleased at the answers.

Again I wondered why Kate should keep Tom on a leash as regards cash. I wondered what his reaction should be if I was to disclose all Kate's assets.

I was beginning to think it was time to confront Kate with what I knew. This boy didn't have to have a partner. Yet I was glad that it was I and no other whom he'd come to talk to that day.

There was some mystery and I was determined to know what it was.

There was certainly no mother love for Tom. Indeed, there were times when she was downright aggressive as if he had never been accepted as her son...

Maybe she'd never expected old Tom to claim his rights or be capable of fathering a child. Maybe he'd forced himself on her in a last desperate attempt to replace Jed. It was so long ago, that Tom's conception would never be explained.

I jumped at the chance of riding alone

with her when she approached me one day when I was bored and Tom was away on his own business. Now I should find an excuse to bring up the subject I wanted to talk about.

We rode in silence for a long while. She too, must have had things on her mind. I was enjoying the familiar rolling pastures, the hills we'd known when we'd come back from the war, sick in mind and body and old Tom had told us to take our time and heal ourselves before we got back to the job of helping to run the ranch. I saw the tree stump that was left after Jed and I sawed the old tree down to make fence posts for another corral. We'd had such great ideas of improving on old Tom's tried and proved methods for getting the beeves to market.

We'd all had such plans, all three of us, and it was as if Kate Beamish had come along and tossed a hand grenade square in amongst us three.

My reverie was interrupted by a shot and by damn it wasn't many inches from my ear!

I looked round for Kate, but she was lagging behind ... well behind. Startled, my horse did a bit of rearing and I swore. My old legs weren't so good in emergencies. Chicago wasn't the best place to keep up good riding habits. Another shot and I reacted as I should have done long years ago. But this time I just fell off with a thump that had no spring in it and rolled, shaken behind a lump of scrub.

I yelled to Kate to duck but she was acting very calm and then it struck me, the bitch was setting me up.

I had my trusty old Colt strapped to my waist but no rifle in the boot. I never anticipated someone taking potshots on Bar C land. I cursed and snapped off two shots in the general direction of the trees on my right and from the point I reckoned the bastard was firing from.

Then I saw Kate riding away hell for leather and I was being left to whoever she trusted to shoot my lights out. My mind slid to the bald man, Sam. He was the shifty-eyed individual with the egg-head who gave me a surly answer when I spoke to him. He was Kate's foreman and no friend of Tom's. I would wager my last year's income from the meat-packing plant to a horse-ball that he was the one out there, sizing me up for a pine box.

The horse I was riding, panicked and galloped off. I estimated that I was three good riding hours from the ranch. I was in a pickle. I was good as dead unless I could use some good old-fashioned know-how. At least I knew the terrain.

Sam, if it was he, had no idea I knew where the gulleys were, or the shortcuts through the hills or the cave half a mile farther down the valley, where I could fort up if I could but reach it.

I bellied my way through the long grass. Fortunately it was at the right time of year and the cows had not eaten all before them. No slugs came my way so he couldn't see what I was up to, but neither could I see what he was doing. It was a game of cat and mouse.

I reached a group of boulders and collapsed on my belly while my old heart pounded and jumped. Then feeling a little better, I hunkered up and took a quick looksee. All was quiet. There was no egghead coming after me.

I waited for a while and my heart slowed to normal but my legs felt like jelly as I edged my way forward. I knew what I was looking for, a crack that only a man and a horse could walk through with some difficulty. I doubted if Sam would even know of it.

At last I was viewing it with triumph. The old brain cells weren't letting me down. I moved cautiously through it and in the space of ten minutes I was through it and only a disturbed bird saw my passing.

I was now in amongst a vast tract of land that was like a natural corral. Indeed, there were several small groups of cattle grazing. A bull looked up but went on grazing peacefully beside his cows and calves.

I moved towards the hidden cave. I could hole up and wait for someone to come looking for me. I was too old to go rampaging around looking for some more limber guy who could pick me off at leisure out here on the lone range with nothing but the sun and wind and grazing cows and the odd lizard that slithered away as I stealthily approached.

But my hopes were dashed when another shot bounced off the rocks some way off. The bastard must have known about that crack. Sam was more astute than I'd given him credit for. I cursed and fairly bounded into the cave. At least the bastard would have to come after me and he would be blinded by the darkness but I should see his silhouette...

Once again I was wrong. It wasn't Sam who had followed me through the crack but the youth who followed Kate about with such sick slavish adoration and whom she called Willi and was at Sam's beck and call. Where Willi was, there would be Sam.

Willi was a slow-witted youth and now he rose up out of the grass to see where I had disappeared to. I could have killed him although he was just a little too far out of the

Colt's range. Anyhow, I wasn't a good shot these days. I saw that I was going to have to get away on my own a bit and practise potting tin cans ... if I survived today. Anyhow, it wasn't his fight and I couldn't blame the boy for doing what he was told, especially as he regarded Kate as some kind of goddess.

He waved, facing south, and I presumed that Sam would be coming at the gallop. I was ready. I hunkered down inside the cave behind a smooth boulder. At some time the cave must have been an outlet for storm water thousands of years ago for all the boulders were waterworn.

I waited.

No need to advertise where I was. Let them come and find me. I saw Sam arrive and there was a powwow and Willi pointed to my cave mouth. Sam shook his head. I hoped he wasn't going to act brave. I didn't want to kill or maim any man.

Again I waited and now I was conscious of the heat and thirst. Maybe they hoped to drive me out if they waited long enough.

But I knew time was against them. Tom would come home and Amy knew that I had ridden out with Kate and Kate would have to come up with some mighty good explanations as to why she came home alone.

Suddenly they both moved in, Sam ahead, and I could see the top of his shiny pate for the cave was on higher ground. Willi moved a little to his left so that I was hard put to watch what both were up to.

Then Sam snapped off a couple of shots with his Winchester. I heard the peculiar whine of the slugs as they snarled past into the murky darkness. I was in danger of a ricocheted bullet catching me unawares, so I saved my fire and made as small a ball of myself as I was able while watching what they were up to.

Maybe if I refrained from firing Sam would think Willi had made a mistake and that I'd skedaddled some place else.

The bastard kept up his riflefire and was acute enough to keep out of Colt range, as he hopefully raked the place I should be.

Then tiring of that sport, and perhaps thinking he might have made a hit, he moved in and came like a clumsy buffalo with Willi close behind him.

Then I up and let him have it and I had the satisfaction of seeing blood spout from a head wound. Sam's scream was like that of a jackal whose balls bad been caught in a trap.

Willi dragged him away and I put a shot up his backside to help him but hadn't the satisfaction of hitting him.

But now my blood was up and I followed. It was Sam I was gunning for. I wished I'd busted his head like a melon instead of a graze that would only give him a headache.

I watched as he stood up groggily with Willi supporting him, his eyes in his pale face like two pissholes in the snow. I aimed carefully but Sam collapsed and Willi couldn't hold him as I let off another shot but the slug passed harmlessly over them both.

Then just as I was taking careful aim again, I heard the shouting and Tom and some of the other hands were galloping towards us as if the devil was after them.

I was suddenly weak with relief and my gun arm dropped so that I could hardly grasp the heavy weapon.

They were crowding round Sam and Willi and one of the men was staunching Sam's wound and Tom was looking around, puzzled.

Then I came out of the shadows and walked down the gradient towards him.

'Mr Williams! Thank God you're alive! Ma said you'd both been fired on by those blasted renegade Indians who've been troubling our range for weeks. She blames Ripple being with us. They're wanting her back to punish her for going with a white man. Did you see any of them?'

His open honest face was full of concern. How could I tell him his mother's story was a load of lies? She was depending on Sam's skill in shooting me down with no evidence to show how I'd died. It was just unfortunate that I was still alive and Sam out of any more conflict. As for Willi, Sam had probably given him some yarn about Kate being in danger from me and the boy would think he was protecting the woman who had befriended him. Youths of Willi's calibre could be told anything and they would believe it, even that the moon was a lump of green cheese.

I didn't really know how to answer Tom, so I lied and said that the would-be assailant had got away because Sam and Willi had heard the gunfire and come to see what it was all about and the Indians had fled.

That yarn would keep Kate on her toes because she would know I was lying along with herself and her two henchmen. I wondered what her next trick would be and why she'd taken these extraordinary steps to eliminate me. Surely the crazy woman didn't expect Tom to inherit all my wealth just because of that contract and the fact that I had no children?

One thing was sure: she had a damn good reason for wanting me bumped off.

The look in her eyes tickled a touch of hysteria far inside me. I laughed fit to split my britches when I was finally escorted home along with Sam and Willi and she never visibly relaxed until after she'd been told of Sam and Willi's exploits in driving away a band of Indians and rescuing my good self.

She gave me a good old-fashioned sideways glance but as I went along with the yarn, she could say no more. I grinned at her.

She knew I knew what she knew that I knew, and she could only tut-tut and berate Tom for keeping Ripple in the house.

'I've told you before, and I'll say it again, no good will come from keeping that girl with us. You indulge Amy far too much, Tom. She should be giving Sophie white woman's milk. It's an insult. What do you think Sophie is going to think when she's old enough to understand that her own mother wouldn't breast feed her? If I'm still alive, I'll make damn sure she knows how she treated her. You would think Amy didn't want the child!'

'Mother! Will you shut up? You have no idea what you're talking about. Ripple is kind and good and looking after the baby with Amy and she's doing a good job.'

'But the milk! That child's getting second-class Indian milk! She should be having the best!'

Tom sighed.

'God forgive me! Mother, I've told you before, milk is milk. In Carolina white babies used to be brought up on Negro milk and probably still are. Don't you understand? Ripple is Amy's friend as well as a servant, and she loves all the children. We couldn't possibly have a better person to look after them. Now, please, go and lie down and calm yourself or you will be ill and we don't want that, do we?'

He looked at me still harassed.

'Forgive all this, Mr Williams. I'm afraid Ma does run on sometimes. She's got a bee in her bonnet about employing Indians.'

'Methinks she gets many bees in her bonnet,' and we both grinned like schoolboys with a secret.

Kate did not come down for the evening meal and stayed in her room for the next three days. She blamed the shock of having Indians on the loose on our range but privately I thought she couldn't come and face me for what she knew I knew.

There would have to be a reckoning however, and I was waiting for it.

I had also figured that the time was right to organize a round-up, do some branding and sort out the cattle ready for shipment. It would get some much needed cash into the Bar C account so that Tom was putting up front the equivalent of what I had advanced him. I was itching to see some return on the money and if we didn't get a good sized herd sent up to Chicago we should lose our contracts back east if we couldn't deliver.

Tom was a bit slow on these things like dates and contracts. Believe me, he had a lot to learn and I was determined to see he got a crash course. Living under his mother's thumb had done him a piece of no-good.

Sam was still keeping close to the bunk-house even though I'd seen him around with a bloody bandage on his head. Willi danced after Kate and spent a good bit of time driving her into Abilene after she decided to leave her sick bed. It was another way to keep out of my way.

So when Tom organized the round-up I went along to help out as they were two men short. I enjoyed it. It took me back years and after the first few days feeling stiff, I got back into the swing of things. We camped out and old Pegleg Hans who was the Bar C wrangler and looked after the Coggins blood horses, proved to be a good cook. As the herd grew bigger as they were chivvied from out of the gulleys and scrub, the nightly sounds of singing took over. There was a happy atmosphere about the men. Tom was a good boss, given the chance to work at his own pace and not interfered with by his ma.

I was pleased by the tally and the beeves

were in better shape than I bargained for. It wasn't a fortune-making herd, but it was useful.

Two nights before we figured to start the drive after turning back milk cows and calves, and those considered wormy or too scrawny, Tom and I were busy figuring up the tally with the idea of being ready to make for the railway sidings. We knew two days would see us underway. We were satisfied and Tom broke out the whiskey to celebrate a good job well done and the boys joined in. All that is, except those who were acting as nighthawks. They would get their ration on the morrow.

The fire was low and half the bottles were empty when all hell broke loose and we rolled out from under our blankets with a curse.

There was an ominous roar, faint but very real and a vibration I'd felt once before and never forgot. Guns cracked and spat and I figured they were on the other side of the herd.

'What in hell...?' Tom clutched my shoulder. The muffled roar was now so bad that he yelled into my ear. 'They're on the hoof! We've got to turn them on the great Buffalo Pasture!'

'No!' I yelled. 'Up on the Great Ridge. They'll wear themselves out running uphill and then we can turn them so they run in on themselves. If they get into their stride on the Buffalo, they'll run forever!'

Tom gave me a strange look but nodded. It figured. Uphill would knock the stuffing out of them. On the flat and they would pound away for miles.

I counted eight hands scrabbling for rearing horses, snorting with fright as the stench of five thousand stampeding head of cattle hit their nostrils. There were saddles to throw aboard and buckles to tighten and then we were off moving away and around and guiding the leaders as they thundered in our direction.

There was no time to plot out any action. It was just enough to follow and wait for the first hesitance as the leaders slowed down to get their second wind.

I saw Tom surrounded by cows as he tried to turn the herd. Three hands followed him and I was following on the outside waiting for mavericks who might have fresh ideas on where to head.

So I was the only one at our side of the herd who suddenly realized we were not alone. A lone horseman was firing point blank into the herd. I cursed. Now of course it was clear. It hadn't been a spooky cow that had set the herd off, it was this man whoever he was, and he was making sure that the herd kept on the run.

I followed him, risking death by crushing to keep after him. I had my lariat rope with me. Now this is a skill I never lost. It had stood me in good stead many a time down at the stockyards when I wanted to examine an individual cow.

The horse under me stretched out his legs and went. He was an experienced cow horse and as soon as I whirled the lariat the horse dug in his heels and dragged backwards. I was lucky. The lariat dropped fair and square over the stranger's head, his hat fell off and I saw the bastard was wearing a kerchief over his face.

I didn't have to see his face however. He was as bald as a coot. Old Sam had been out doing his stuff on the orders of Kate. I could bet money on it.

But something happened, I didn't figure. I yanked him hard and he tried to break free and at the same time he took a snap shot which missed. Then there was a scream and he plunged into a thundering mass of galloping beeves.

There was nothing I could do.

In ten minutes he would be minced-up beef.

Ten minutes after that and he would be just a stain on the ground.

I was sickened. Kate Beamish Coggins had a lot to answer for. But why?

I still couldn't figure it.

There was one comfort in all this. I

wouldn't have to watch my back no more ... not from his angle anyway. I wondered how many more fool-minded cowboys were being influenced by that frail-looking woman who had the mind and heart of a cougar?

I watched helplessly as the cows thundered on until at last I sensed that they were slowing down. I fell back, my horse quivering and snorting until we were well clear and I left Tom and the hands with the heartbreaking task of rounding up that vast herd again.

Suddenly I had no heart for checking and counting beeves. There was something far more important to do.

It was showdown time.

Time to put all cards on the table.

Kate Beamish versus Lofty Williams.

I knew it would be a fight to the death...

## FIVE

She was sat rocking in her own special chair on the veranda when I returned. Her old arthritic hands grasped the arms so fiercely that they showed white bones.

She sat like a scrawny black spider.

Slowly I dismounted. My old bones ached and my mind sickened and weary. Then I stood before her, looking up at her hunched figure. She saw the truth in my eyes.

'I've been waiting for you.' Her voice had lost its thrusting arrogance.

I nodded.

'I'm not easy to kill, Kate.'

She moved uneasily, stiffly, as if her own bones hurt.

'I made a mistake. I should have done it myself as soon as I realized...'

'Realized what, Kate?'

'That Mr Williams, the meat-packing king' – and now there was a trace of a sneer in the cracked voice – 'was in reality my old friend, Lofty, who killed Jed, and is still a fugitive from the law, I might add!'

'Is that a threat?'

She chuckled. 'It could be. You did very well for yourself, Lofty. I didn't recognize you before you shaved off that beard. It was quite a shock. A ghost from the past, you might say.'

'I wondered about that. You were good at hiding your feelings. You had me fooled, Kate. At least it answers the question of why you put your dogs on me.'

She nodded pensively.

'I'd my reasons, but not those that might spring to your mind. My reasons are private.'

'To protect your family?'

She gave a start.

'What do y'know...?' Then she stopped and bit her lip and she did the pursing of the duck's arse bit. 'You'll not trick me into talking, Lofty Williams!'

I shrugged painful shoulders.

'I know all I need to know. It's time for a reckoning, Kate. I should kill you for what you made me do to Jed!'

'It was an accident, Lofty. I never meant you to kill him!'

I fumbled my gun and then dragged it out and cocked it. I never was a one for a fast draw and now I was more clumsy than ever.

'Lofty! I swear...'

'For God's sake, Kate, don't risk your rotten soul in hell by swearing. I wouldn't believe a word you said, not if you had your hand clasped with the Lord's!'

Her eyes slid every which way and her face grew waxen white until I thought she was going to faint on me. My lips came back in a snarl.

'Come on now, Kate, where's that big-hearted courage of yours? I think you could at least stand up to face what's coming to you.'

She made a mighty visible effort to control herself.

'What about Amy and the children? Do you want to shock them?'

Amy and the children? I had forgotten them in my sickened hate and confusion. Hell! They mustn't suffer for my fury and satisfaction in blasting Kate Beamish.

I hesitated and lowered the heavy gun and that was my mistake.

Her eyes slid far past me.

'Take him, Pete, and blast him good!' and the frail old voice strengthened, fed on venom and rage.

I turned and moved quicker than I had done for years and the sight behind me turned my knees to jelly and I dropped like a stone which actually saved my life, for the slug whistled overhead like an angry hornet.

The old man before me was using an ancient Paterson I suspected, a clumsy model that made firing difficult. I had time to wriggle away but I didn't. I sprang behind Kate and dragged her light frame in front of me.

The old man stood helpless, his brains paralysed.

'Hell, Kate! What do we do now?' he quavered and I could feel Kate's body tremble beneath my grasp.

She was violently angry and the new strength in her voice was like a whiplash.

'Go and find Joshua, you old fool! He'll know what to do!' And I stood holding her like a fool.

Suddenly they were all around me, three, four of them and I wondered who the hell they were.

And where were Amy and the kids?

Kate regained her poise and sat down, already mistress of the situation. God, how I wished I'd killed her on sight rather than give in to the temptation of goading her beforehand.

Joshua hassled me away from her, holding my hands behind my back as easily as if I was a baby. He was a big, beer-gutted feller strong in the shoulders and back and reminded me of someone used to breaking rocks. His hard shovel-hands pushed hard into my back and I let myself be handled like a sack of corn. I was too old to square up to a man of his kind.

Kate's beady eyes were upon me.

'In case you're wondering, the family's locked up in the children's bedroom.'

'But why? What's all this about, Kate? What's happening?'

She gave a tired smile, and then gave a long sigh.

'I can't help any of this any more than you can, Lofty. That old man looking bewildered and lost is my husband.' I turned and looked at the little scarecrow with shock and I could hardly take in her words. 'He's done his time in the pen and now he's out and he and his one-time pards are here to suck me dry! How's that for an ironic joke?'

'But...' I began, for my brains were a little slow to take in the implications. She nodded.

'Yes, that's right. Pete, here is my legitimate husband. Tom Coggins was never my husband.'

‘And Tom…?’

‘Is a bastard. Now you know the truth or part of the truth!’

My old brains whirled. Jesus Christ! That woman had sat on the Bar C for more than forty years depriving me of my rights as Tom Coggins’s adopted son as well as manipulating me to kill Jed. My fury ate into me like a canker. It was acid and burned my stomach.

‘What should I do with him?’ I heard fat-belly Joshua ask.

‘He’s no threat. Put him in with the family and then we’ll get on with the plans. I’ve already been to the bank…’

My ears flapped as I was being bundled away. Bank? What the hell did she need to go to the bank for?

Tom and I and the hands had been away more than a week on the round-up, what had that devil woman been up to?

I had no time to form theories. I was thrust into the room with a savage push to the back and the door slammed behind me.

I fell on my knees.

Gentle hands raised me. Amy's eyes were red with weeping but now she was calm, I suspect for the children's sake and that of Ripple.

I looked about. Ripple hugged the sleeping babe while the two boys played with the train set and Annie absorbed herself in changing her doll's clothes. Picture-books were scattered on the floor too as if Amy had busied herself in keeping the children's minds off the strange situation.

There was also food and a large pitcher of water. We weren't going to be deprived of creature comforts.

'What's been going on here?' I managed to gasp when I'd got over my fall.

Amy's lips trembled.

'She was being more obnoxious than usual. I've always dreaded Tom being away. She's never wanted me to be here. She was against our marriage in the first place and each time there was a baby she made it quite clear she didn't welcome them. It's been a dreadful time but now...' She sniffed into her handkerchief.

'Yes? Come on, Amy, let's have it all.' For the first time I was irritated by Amy's timidity. It didn't bring out the protective instinct in me, rather the opposite.

'Last night the men came. She wasn't expecting them. I'd overheard her talking to Sam much earlier and she wanted him to hinder the round-up and during the confusion finish the job he'd already been paid to do. I didn't really know what she was talking about but it sounded bad. I tackled her about it and she was in a fine rage. She struck me. The children were already in bed with Ripple watching them. Sam was already long gone because I couldn't pluck up courage for a long while to face her.'

'But you finally did. Go on.'

'I was shocked and holding my cheek and she picked up a domed glass with wax flowers inside it, and flung it at me. It broke against the wall and a piece of glass cut my hand. She screamed she would kill me.

Then … we both heard horses in the yard, and she forgot me and hurried outside. I thought it was Tom and you come home and I rushed out too. I wanted Tom's arms about me and to let him know once and for all, just how his mother treats me when we're alone.'

'And they were these men?'

'Yes, a little old man and a big fellow they called Joshua and three other men I didn't like the look of. The old man seemed to be frightened of this Joshua too. I was frightened and tried to go back inside, but one of the men stopped me by pointing his gun at me and telling me to be a good girl.'

'Did Mrs Coggins recognize any of them?'

'Yes. The little old man. She called him Pete and she got quite a shock to see him. She said she thought that he would have been dead by now and wanted to know what he wanted.'

'And what did he want?'

'Money, a place to stay and a place to hide the men with him. That everyone at the ranch had to be got rid of, that a hiding-place had to be found for Ned, who would kick the pen in about a month's time. The plans were already in action...'

'Ned? Now who the hell's Ned?' Amy shook her head, and my mind raced. 'Kicking the pen is he? That means Ned, whoever he is, is going to break out.' And as I looked at Amy's puzzled face, it hit me. Whoever was breaking out was to use the Bar C as a hiding-place! Then how would that leave Tom and the others and this family?

My heart jumped into my throat. I didn't react to shocks of this sort very well. I wasn't cast into a heroic mould, anyway. But I kept my thoughts to myself. Amy had enough to worry about without all the possibilities I was cooking up.

Talking of cooking...

'What about something to eat?' I asked it in a tone that made her jump.

'Of course, I'm sorry. I didn't think. We've got water and a little beer and Mrs Coggins saw to it we had food. It's more in keeping with what the children eat, I'm afraid.'

'But it's food and we must keep up our strength.'

'Mr Williams,' she said fearfully as she cut and buttered bread and piled it high with cold salted bacon, 'why did you come back? Does it mean Tom will soon be here too?'

I hesitated. This was no time to tell her about Sam and the stampede and whatever was happening out there. I didn't even know if Tom and the others were all in one piece after that savage breakneck charge.

'Look, Amy, I came back because I came off my horse and I'm too old for all the rough stuff. I should never have gone on that round-up. Now take it easy, Amy. You know Tom will come back when he's done the job he set out to do. Right?'

She nodded doubtfully and handed me a platter piled high with doorstep sandwiches.

Ripple sat silent and still but taking in all that was said. Then while I was eating she said softly, 'I can get out of the window and climb down to the ground and I can go and find Mr Tom and tell him what's happening here.'

Amy looked horrified while I was thoughtful. Then I shook my head.

'With the best will in the world, you'll never find them in time.' And I told them of the real situation and that the herd had thundered miles back into the scrub and that it would put extra days on to the round-up.

Amy started to weep and suddenly I sympathized with Kate who'd had to live with Amy's timidity and fears. For a woman of Kate's calibre, Amy would be beneath contempt.

'Hush, Amy, you're going to panic the children.' They had all stopped what they were doing and were staring at their mother. Already Annie's underlip was trembling. 'Listen carefully and I'll tell you what we're going to do.'

They listened in silence, Ripple nodding and Amy, apprehensive. Then when I'd finished, she said, all panicky like, 'But we can't do that! They're only babies. How can we take them all the way to that cave?'

'There's no alternative. You said yourself that this Ned feller is coming here to make this place his hideout. How many times a year do you get visitors? None; I thought not,' as Amy shook her head. 'The Bar C could be burned off the face of the earth and no one in Abilene any the wiser. This Ned feller could hole up here for years!'

'But the children could never walk the distance!'

Ripple turned black eyes on to Amy and then myself.

'I could go first and find horses. There's George's pony in the corral. He and Harry could ride together and I could lead them. You, sir, could carry the baby on horseback and you, ma'am could hold Annie in front of you.'

I nodded. I wasn't sure about handling tiny babies and it was a bad time to find out but I couldn't shirk now.

Swiftly Amy and Ripple packed up food and water and some mysterious things that would be needed for the baby. They were all put into two bundles and then we got round to the serious business of getting Ripple out of the window and down to the ground.

The time was right. We could smell roasting beef, the smell coming from the cookhouse so Kate was bestirring her stumps for once and cooking herself. Then there was a time of silence punctuated by laughter and Ripple went for it and climbed down like a cat.

There was a nail-biting wait and then Ripple was there under the window, and a faint call of an owl alerted us.

Now it was going to be now or never time. If the baby cried, then we would be in the shit good and proper. But for once, Amy had put ethics on one side and with a hint of defiance given her baby daughter a draught of water laced with whiskey. The little one slept like the dead.

The other children were too scared to cry. Indeed, George, who was three years older than Harry thought it was no end of a lark having his ma lifting her petticoats and showing a lot of black stocking as she clambered clumsily over the window-sill and grabbed the hand-holds as we helped her down.

I lifted each child down in a kind of hammock made from a blanket off one of the beds. The baby went down last, swaying like a bundle of hay and Amy clasped her tightly to her bosom as if she would never let go again.

Then, puffed and already exhausted I was down too and I couldn't get them all to the tethered horses fast enough. Ripple had used her noddle and they were ready saddled behind the blacksmith's shop.

Kate and those eating and drinking with her, never heard us go. We stole away and even the children had enough sense to keep their tongues still.

I described the cave again and Ripple said she knew of it. There was very little the Indians didn't know about this land that was theirs in the old days. She also knew a more direct route and I thought I knew that range like the back of my hand.

She was right. It cut a couple of hours off the time even though we travelled at a snail's pace because of Ripple walking beside the boys' pony.

Strange thoughts and feelings went through me as I hugged baby Sophie to me. Her warm little body snuggled against my heart. I was conscious of a great loss. I should have married again after I lost Bonny. It would have felt good to know that part of one would live forever in the bodies of any descendants. Having no family of my own meant that when I was dead, everything about me would be dead. Full stop.

It was cold and dark in that cave just as I remembered it. At least they were safe. The boys chased around, playing games but Annie hated it. She'd brought her doll with her which was a comfort, I suppose. She sat close to her ma and the baby, when Ripple wasn't tanking the greedy little glutton up.

I scouted around a little, and set a few

snares and caught me several jackrabbits which were mighty useful. I kept a lookout but no one seemed to be looking for us.

But time and patience were running short, we had to know what was happening and where was Tom and the herd?

Finally, at the risk of Sophie not getting her tank of milk, I reluctantly sent Ripple off to find her folks after making sure that no harm would come to her on sight.

I'd become fond of Ripple. She was as near a Christian as an Indian could be. She had sense and heart and she was loyal. She regarded Amy and the children as her family.

I took her hand in mine.

'You're sure now, your people will accept you?'

'Yes, I'm sure. Mr Tom had been a good friend of my tribe over the years, giving beef during famine times. Old Mrs Coggins would not get help but Mr Tom's family will be helped. I swear it.'

'Good. Then there is no time to waste. Tell

them how we are placed here and that we wait for Mr Coggins's return. He and his men should be returning from Abilene if all has gone as it should.'

I considered telling her to send a message to the marshal at Abilene about this Ned, and thought better of it. I scribbled a note torn from the flyleaf of a prayerbook I always carried with me … it was a gift from Bonny when we married and she was very proud because she had given me a real printed book.

Ripple watched me write and nodded when I said softly, 'Send this to Mr Tom so that it is a warning what to expect back at the ranch.'

'Shall I tell him about his mother?'

'I have explained everything. Now go.'

I went inside the cave. Amy's face was drawn. She had no milk of her own and now her worry was for the baby. I hoped and prayed Ripple would find her tribe quickly, send her message and return hopefully with food and blankets and maybe one or two loyal bucks who could forage for us and keep a lookout.

For I was sadly tired now. The responsibility and the very struggle for survival was sucking the life out of me. I dreaded becoming a burden on Amy. I couldn't become a burden … I had to summon every ounce of energy and willpower to carry me through.

There was also something else sucking the life out of me, the anger and rage of Kate Beamish and that little man she said was her legal husband. I wanted to kill them both. The anger was an actual pain in my gut like an ulcer eating into me, not letting up for an instant.

Amy had found a spring. It oozed out of the ground somewhere beyond the cave. She was in the habit of going there every day to do her own toilet and to wash the few diapers that they'd brought with them for Sophie. She struggled in vain to keep the other three clean. From being well-mannered, well-dressed youngsters they were now looking like any ragtag kids from the muddy streets of Abilene.

Two days after Ripple left us, she went to the spring to wash. Sophie had diarrhoea because of the change from milk. Amy had tried her with thin broth saved from cooking a jackrabbit, and thickened it with some of the hard stale bread crumbed up. The greedy baby had taken it well enough, but later had screamed with bellyache and then had come the distressing diarrhoea and Amy had panicked.

Now the child was sleeping and Amy was making up for lost time. These last few days since Ripple had gone, Amy's character had stiffened, she was a very different woman now to the girl who had been frightened of her mother-in-law and leaned on the Indian girl.

I was watching the fire and the pot sitting precariously on the flames and the other children were gathered around it and Annie was dutifully watching the baby. I had time to think of Kate and that little runt of a feller who was her husband. It was plain now why Kate had come to Abilene from San Francisco. She'd been destitute and probably on the run. She'd been looking for a rich husband and a place to hide, and she must have made up her mind to have old Tom, the moment Jed took her home as the reluctant Tom's housekeeper. Jed's fate had been sealed when he'd first laid eyes on her, as was my own, in the sense of losing all that which I should have shared with Jed.

I was roused from my brooding reverie by a scream.

The children looked up, startled. I stopped them from springing up and running to their mother. I grabbed up the sleeping baby and rushed them all inside the cave.

'Stay there, whatever you do. If you disobey me, I'll skin your arses!' I thrust the baby in George's arms. 'Sit,' I said tersely, 'and keep out of sight!' and I was away, moving as fast as my stiff old legs would take me.

I was shocked to recognize one of Joshua's men. It hadn't occurred to me that someone might eventually find us. He was holding her by the hair in a cruel grip that forced her head backwards. He was in the act of kissing her throat when I came upon them. As I watched, I heard her bodice rip as she struggled in vain to free herself.

'Hold it!' I sounded more fierce than I really was. 'Let her go, or I'll blow your head off!'

For a moment I thought he was going to do as I said, but then his eyes narrowed and he pulled her in front of him.

'Go on, shoot, old man, and you'll kill her,' and he laughed, an unpleasantly shrill laugh.

It was stalemate.

'You think I won't?' I was hard put not to sound trembly.

'I don't think, old 'un. I know you won't, not if you value this 'ere woman's life.'

I took a deep breath and for the first time for years, I said a prayer … and I aimed for the top of his head.

There was a scream and a streak of red as

I scalped him good and proper. Amy fell away from him as he crumpled and fell in slow motion, an extraordinary look of astonishment widening his dead eyes and opening the now silent mouth.

I strode forward without a word and pulled the sobbing Amy to her feet.

'You all right?' She nodded, burrowing her head into my chest. Suddenly I felt ten feet tall and damn me, if my aches and pains hadn't but damn all vanished!

I helped her back to the cave and she lay down for a while after I gave her a shot of our precious small supply of liquor. Later, she calmed down and contrived to knot her ripped bodice so that she was respectable.

I took the children on a ramble near where I had laid some snares. The boys came upon two rabbits and they were as overjoyed as if they had laid the snares themselves. I was finding much pleasure in their company. Only Annie was a little quiet. She had not forgotten the scream or the echoing shot and every now and again looked apprehensively around. She was missing her father. I hoped it wouldn't be long before we were once again united for I was uneasy about him too. I faced the fact that I should be devastated if anything happened to that fine young feller.

Late that night, I dug a shallow grave and laid the gory remains to rest. I contemplated the grave. Soon, the stranger would be missed and Joshua and his men come looking for him. We'd be lucky if we escaped the hunt. It was sure time to move but where to?

Ripple had the answer. The next day, she arrived with four bucks, food and two travois pulled by two Indian ponies. The pole and skin contraptions were already furnished so that Amy and the baby and Annie could travel in one and the boys and Ripple in the other. I was to ride alongside.

We ate a hearty meal and lit no fire and then we scattered the dead ashes and one of the bucks brushed all around the cave so that there was no sign. He also visited the spring and did likewise and then went and examined the grave. This too, he obliterated and unless there was an Indian tracker with Joshua, that body would never be discovered.

We moved out and was I pleased! I'd never been so glad to see Indians in my life as I did at that time.

The chief had sent a runner to find Tom, and was even now scouring the country between here and Abilene and following the cattle trail.

So I took heart. Tom would come a'running when he finally got the message. What he should do about his mother, I had no idea. I hoped he would do nothing. I wanted to deal with her myself.

## SIX

My spine prickled. The hairs on the back of my neck stirred and lifted as I slowly rode past the small group of Indians who stood silently watching our arrival. Cheyennes! It had been years since I'd faced Indians, and then it hadn't been in friendship.

Now, these Cheyenne relatives of Ripple's watched impassively, accepting us but not welcoming us.

I saw Amy peeping from under a blanket and she too looked apprehensive and clutched Sophie closer to her.

But we need not have feared. When our little cavalcade finally stopped outside the chief's lodge, we could not have had a better welcome. Chief Chocata was a tall well-set up old man and the burden of years sat well on him. I reckoned him to be one of the most honest and proudest men I'd ever had the privilege to meet. He was not corrupted by white man's ways or liquor or the dubious lust for gold.

Certainly he was a renegade. He had tried the reservation and found it a death in life. So, he had made a decision and led his people back into the wilderness and over the years they had lived in the inaccessible wild places with very little communication with white men. They had kept out of trouble and so could come and go as they pleased.

The exception had been Tom Coggins. He had allowed them cows during the bad years. Kate had disapproved but for once Tom had overruled her. It had been the friendship with the Bar C folk that had sent Ripple astray. She had met and lain with a lone hunter who had stayed for a while during the branding season. But he had moved on and Ripple with him. They had settled in a shack just outside Abilene and he took temporary jobs with the smaller ranchers or the trail bosses bringing in the herds to the railroads.

Ripple had found out the hard way that all a squaw was for, was for beating, making love to like an animal, feeding her man and putting him to bed when he came home drunk from the saloons in Abilene.

It all came to an end when he was shot down in a drunken brawl and she was kicked out of the miserable shack as an undesirable.

She was too proud to go back to her tribe. Indeed, she knew she would not be welcome, and it was only after the baby was born and she was found nearly dead by a Bar C cowhand and taken to the ranch, that Chief Chocata relented. He watched from afar as the girl became the white woman's companion and second mother to the little white papoose. That, he was proud of.

So now, he stepped out to greet us in stately dignity. I sensed he was happy to discharge an obligation to the Coggins family.

'Welcome to my lodge, and welcome too, to the friend of Water-That-Ripples-Over-Stones, and her children. You will be safe here. The drums tell us that there are strangers on the land taken by Tom Coggins.'

I told him about the man Joshua and the men with him and also about the man in the lonely grave. He nodded gravely.

'And what of the old woman chief? Does she approve of this?'

I lifted my shoulders.

'I don't know. Your guess is as good as mine. She certainly knew one man with them but whether she is a prisoner or not, I do not know. But Tom Coggins is in danger, that I do know.'

The chief raised his eyebrows.

'But he is the woman chief's son! How can he be in danger?'

'Again, I cannot say, but it is so.'

I stood wooden, unyielding as I watched astonishment and disbelief on the carved mask of a face. He, this proud wild man was thinking that it was we, the white men who were the savages and it was hard to understand.

At last he gestured and Amy and the children were unloaded from the travois and taken into the chief's lodge and tended by his womenfolk.

I myself was allowed to wander freely as Chief Chocata pondered on what was to do. He powwowed with his bucks and then sought me out. I was sitting under a tree trying to fathom out Kate and her strange behaviour.

Chief Chocata stood before me and greeted me formally as if we had not spoken some two hours previously. Then he sat down abruptly facing me, cross-legged and straight-backed. He drew a filthy smelling pipe from under his breechclout and proceeded to charge it and then taking a box of white man's lucifers from the same place, lit the smelly concoction. He drew in smoke with evident enjoyment and got it going well and then offered it to me.

I daren't refuse. It was a gesture of trust and friendship. I drew in smoke, let it roll around my mouth and blew out with gusto. He smiled and nodded and when I returned it, inhaled again and then put the pipe aside. The formalities were over.

'We have come to a decision after much talk. We shall look after Tom Coggins's woman and her children but we shall not sound the war drums. We have lived in peace since long before my young braves were born. It is not the time to go against the white man's law.'

I nodded. I could follow his reasoning. This wasn't his fight.

'Therefore, because Tom Coggins and his family showed compassion to a foolish member of our tribe and gave her back her honour by trusting her with their own small child, we shall care for his family as if they belonged to the Cheyenne.'

'And what about me?'

Chief Chocata smiled and it was like a piece of ancient wood cracking.

'You are a man and not of the family and so you shall go and seek Tom Coggins. He is already on his way back to the ranch and your note was delivered. It is well that you meet with him and can plan your action. My bucks will not follow you. It is white man's business. You understand?'

'Yeh, you're a great chief, Chief Chocata. In Washington you'd be considered a diplomat!' Chief Chocata nodded and smiled. He didn't know what a diplomat was, but if I said he was one, then he was.

I ate their food, which was peculiar, all tasted up with herbs that I didn't recognize but which I took a shine to. It gave me strength and the home-made liquor coursed down into my stomach and started muffled drums rolling. To this day I don't know whether they put in something special to make me feel ten feet tall. I suspect they did.

However, I rode out ready to do or die.

Chief Chocata's son rode with me part of the way and put me on the right track. All I had to do now was to keep the sun at my back and I should hit Tom Coggins's trail.

I pushed that old horse, and I pushed myself. We were both creaking when I spied a dust cloud on the trail ahead. I was choking in my own dust and the sun beat down until I wasn't sure my old eyes were not playing tricks.

But the Indian had been right about hitting Tom's trail and I drew up and watched Tom and his boys coming at a fair lick considering the heat and all.

I took time to wet my lips from the leather waterbag the Cheyenne womenfolk had given me along with some pemmican and cornbread. I watered the horse too. I didn't want the poor beast dropping under me.

I was ready and waiting when Tom came within hailing distance.

'What's all this about trouble at the ranch, Mr Williams?' he bawled as he hauled in his horse with his hands bunched behind him.

He tipped back his stetson and wiped grease and sweat from his forehead. The hands behind him looked sick as dogs and I concluded that they'd been fast spending their wages after they'd delivered those beeves to the stockyards. Abilene had been a mighty fine place to whoop it up. But for once I wasn't interested in any cash deal I was mixed up in. I couldn't have cared less about Tom's success rate.

I told him what happened in a few words as possible, and he swore long and luridly.

'And you sit there and tell me my own mother actually had my wife and family locked in a bedroom?'

'Yessir! It's just as I tell it. We'd be there yet if it hadn't been for Ripple climbing out of the window and rounding up some horses.'

'And Amy actually climbed out of the window along with the kids? My God, there's going to be some trouble for this!'

I had never seen Tom in such a panpucker and for a quiet even-tempered man he was showing blinding rage that threatened to split him in half. I was glad it wasn't me who would have to square up to him.

We dismounted and took time out from the sun while Tom chewed over the situation. He looked ten years older and I was sorry for him. It must be hell to have a mother like his. Then there was Amy and the kids to worry over.

'So you reckon she and the kids are OK

with the Cheyenne?'

'Yeh. The boys were regarding it as an adventure. They were playing with Chocata's grandchildren when I left and Annie was staying close to her ma and Ripple. That girl's sure a wonder.'

Tom nodded absent-mindedly. It was obvious he was figuring on some course of action.

Then he looked at me very serious.

'And what about this man, Pete, and Ned who's expecting to hole up at the Bar C?'

I had been a bit chary about speaking of Pete. It could be a sore point when Tom realized who he really was. I took a deep breath.

'Your mother knew him before she met your father, but Ned, I have no idea who he is. Maybe he's connected with Joshua who seems to be the leader of the bunch. It's my view they're all prisoners ... ex-prisoners, if you like.'

'You mean this Pete is an ex-prisoner?'

I closed my eyes. It was getting harder and harder.

'Yeh, he's done his time and he was turfed out.'

'But why turn up at the Bar C for God's sake?'

I took a deep breath. He had to know sometime.

'He came looking for your mother. He's her husband, Tom!'

Tom laughed. 'This is no time to joke, Mr Williams.' Then his eyes slitted. 'You're not joking, are you?'

'Nope! As you say, this is no time for jokes.'

For a long moment there was silence as Tom took in all the implications and then he stood up and walked away up a bluff and behind a boulder and then I heard his stentorian roar as he let out his fury.

I watched the hands move about their business of caring for their horses. They knew enough to keep well away from the boss at this time.

The sun was moving well down when he strode back, a dark hidden expression at the back of his eyes. I said nothing but saddled up and the boys followed suit and we waited for Tom. He was slow and deliberate and when he was ready he leaned on his pommel and looked at me.

'I'm going to kill that woman, God help me but I am! As for the feller ... I'm going to drive him and all the other scum from off my place! Are you with me?'

I nodded. I couldn't think of a thing to say.

They were gone when we got to the ranch. The place was deserted and it had been ransacked. I couldn't make my mind up whether Kate had gone willingly or been forced.

Privately, I thought she'd gone willingly when I remembered her reference to the bank. I had the sneaky feeling too, that the money was to do with the springing of Ned whoever he was, out of jail.

This Ned must be some bloody feller, for Kate to give up everything for. You could never figure women. Who would expect a woman to betray her own son and abandon him and his family for a ragged old bastard like Pete and this mystery man, Ned?

Tom left the ranch to go find Amy and the kids and fetch them home. I wasn't too sure it was a good idea for I was thinking when Ned was sprung, they might all hightail it back and this time there would be gunplay. But Tom was adamant. He didn't want Amy and the kids living with the Cheyenne any longer than was necessary.

I spent time putting things to rights but as I didn't really have the knowledge of where things went I could only make the rooms habitable. Amy and Ripple were going to have a lot of clearing up to do.

I cut a slab of beef from a side hanging in the cool house, and I chopped it up small and made stew against their return. This was something I was good at from the old days. I added wild onion and I hooked the blackened pot on to a hook over the open fire and let it simmer. I even made panbread and it brought all the old days back again when Jed and me and old Tom did for ourselves. They were good old days.

Amy flung her arms about me when they all returned safely. She was like a daughter greeting me. Even the kids crowded round and I felt good as Ripple doled out beef and divided up the panbread. It was like being a member of the family.

After Amy and Ripple retired to get the children to bed, Tom produced the bank draft for the beeves.

'I thought you would have settled for cash,' I said gruffly.

'I took a little cash, enough for the hands' back wages and for running the house. The rest is as arranged. I'm sorry it isn't more but the state of the market's not good and neither were the beeves.'

'I'm sorry, boy, they weren't up to my standards or I should have taken them for the plant. As it is, we'll introduce new blood lines and phase out those Mexican steers that are more bone than meat.'

'You're satisfied then, Mr Williams? I'm doing the best I can and if you want to open a new account between us, I'll be proud to work with you.'

I put my hand on his shoulder.

'Boy, I don't trust many people in the meat business, but I trust you as if you were my own flesh and blood!'

Tom flushed. He wasn't a man good with words, so he only nodded and left the room.

We stayed close to home for a few days on the lookout for the gang's return. I couldn't get it out of my mind about what they planned to do. Tom pooh-poohed it and said now they could be far away in Mexico. I know he still brooded about his mother. There was often a faraway look in his eyes.

But finally one day we decided to risk it and go to town. It was getting imperative that I should arrange about a joint account at the bank and send a few telegraphs off to the plant back in Chicago.

Strangely enough, Chicago was becoming a dream to me. After all the turbulent years of making my way and fighting and climbing upwards on the tops of the backs of others, I was now ready to let it all go. I even contemplated selling out to my most dangerous rival.

Tom had business of his own. Amy had been chewing his ear about supplies and cotton goods and linament for George who sometimes suffered from bronchitis.

I had sent my telegraphs and had a chat to the stationmaster and heard that there had been several hold-ups down the line. I pricked up my ears. I didn't like the sound of things. I was on my way to the bank with the draft when I bumped into the town marshal who was a man I didn't take to and only acknowledged when I stepped off the train that first day. Tom had said his name was Rigby.

'Good morning, Marshal.' I was ready to move on. He stopped me fair and square.

'Mr Williams, isn't it?'

'Yeh, that's me.'

'I'm having a word with all strangers to the town. It's a mighty big undertaking but me and my deputies are working through you all.'

'Oh? And why is that, Marshal?'

'Haven't you heard? We've got a sight of robbings going on all around us.'

'Hell's bells! You aren't trying to pin it on to us strangers?'

'Nope! Just wondered if you'd seen anything out of the ordinary on the way here. Seen anyone suspicious on the train coming in, or seen any strangers riding over the Coggins land?'

I was a bit flummoxed. I didn't think Tom would want it known about Kate lighting out with a set of ruffians. Besides, all this rumouring might have nothing to do with our bunch. So it was no good me mouthing off any suspicions. Tom wouldn't think it very friendly.

'Naw ... not a thing,' I mumbled and wondered whether I was wrong to deny any strange happenings. After all, if they came back, we should need all the help we could get.

Marshal Rigby nodded.

'Just as I figured. No one knows a damn

thing, so it must be some out-of-town boys, and I wish to hell they'd go back from where they came from!'

I shuddered inwardly. God forbid that they would return to the Bar C!

I saw Tom elbowing his way through the crowd, his face white, his eyes wild. He caught hold of me.

'What the...?' But he stopped me speaking by jerking me into a narrow alley that ran round the back of the drygoods store.

'What is it?' I managed to gasp for Tom looked like a crazy man.

'I've just been to the bank. I got my stores first so that I could figure on how much to draw. D'you know what?' And his Adam's apple kept working up and down as if his guts was wanting to throw.

'What?' But I had a bloody good idea.

'She's cleaned me out. Our joint account was cleared three days after we left on that round-up! My own mother...!' Suddenly he was crying, huge tearing sobs that tugged at my heart. Each ragged sound punched me in the solar plexus. I put an arm about him but he shrugged me off and turned his back on me.

I stood and waited for the storm of emotion to expend itself. It was like watching a rock splitting from the inside from the pent-up energy in him.

Then, with ravaged face, he faced me.

'I'm going after her, wherever she is, I'll find her, and then...' He didn't finish. He didn't need to.

## SEVEN

Tom had cooled down by the time we returned to the ranch. He warned me not to say anything to Amy. She and Ripple had plenty on their hands looking after the children as well as cooking for the hands.

Amy and the children were on the lookout for us as we came home. It struck me how much freer they all were since Kate's leaving. Amy positively glowed now that she was home and had everything to her liking. Annie too, did not cling so much. It made me wonder if Kate had enjoyed making everyone unhappy. Maybe she had always been an unhappy woman herself.

Now that thought struck a curious chord. Had she always been an unhappy woman? Had she loved that little runt of a man who'd got banged up in the pen?

I tried to think of her as she was when she'd first come to Abilene. I tried to think of her as a laughing carefeee woman but nothing came to mind. But I did remember her being a poised mature person, self-possessed to a degree. Now with hindsight, it might have been a certain pensive charm, an elusive reckless desperation that had attracted Jed's attention in the first place.

It also might have been why there had been so much antagonism as well as attraction between us, all those years ago.

Much later that night I could hear Tom talking to Amy in their bed, and I wondered how much he was telling her.

I had an uneasy foreboding that all was not going too well.

Amy was subdued the next morning. She gave us our steak overdone and the cornbread was burnt. She was as near sulking as ever I'd known her. Tom hadn't put his case too well for why we should go off into the wild blue yonder. She took the view we were abandoning her and the children to their fate, although it had been pointed out that the hands had orders to work around the ranchhouse, just in case...

We rode away early after breakfast and only the boys stood and waved us off. I felt goose-ridden. It was wrong that these two nice people should part in anger. Tom's shoulders slumped. He was a right pig in the middle. On the one hand, his wife angry because he was leaving and on the other, he was gunning for his mother. What a situation for a young feller to be in.

We first rode to the Cheyenne camp. Ripple had given us a tip that Chief Chocata was dealing himself into the game by sending out trackers to hunt for her he called 'the woman chief'.

So we approached the camp not with high hopes but with a kind of desperation. It was a starting point.

Chief Chocata met us with a grin which was surprising as that man never smiled. He held up an arm in greeting.

We responded and got down and a couple

of young bucks took our horses and we settled for a smoke and a powwow.

It seemed that a new white man's outfit was settled in an old log cabin far out on the edge of Bar C land. I looked at Tom enquiringly. Did he know of any such line cabin?

'There are several,' he admitted, 'but I didn't think my mother would know of them. She never rode out very far for as long as I remember. She left searching for strays to the men.'

'Do you know Whitewater Canyon?' Chief Chocata asked quietly and I remembered that in the old days Whitewater Canyon, which was only a small canyon by ordinary standards, was a sacred burial ground of the Cheyenne. A line cabin had been built there but it had been derelict for years for old Tom had always had trouble with the Indians when it was used. No wonder the chief was dealing himself in if they were shacked up there! It also meant we were to have reinforcements. I breathed a sigh of relief. I had imagined Tom and I going thundering in and getting ourselves killed.

Now we had Chief Chocata's skill and native shrewdness and I blessed the day one of the Bar C hands found Ripple and brought her in to become one of the family.

The upshot of the powwow was that the chief and a dozen of his braves would accompany us. The chief's third son would go ahead and take a looksee and then come back and meet us on the way. The track was up in the wild country and we would have to take the roundabout route because of the horses. He would travel on foot and go by the secret Indian trail.

I did consider asking if I could stay in camp, and then thoughts of Kate made that impossible. I'd vowed to see that the old she-cougar got her comeuppance. It wouldn't be right for a son to kill his mother. That was an act against nature.

So I forced my old bones to endure the gruelling ride. I hoped the day would come when I could set on a rocking chair all day and rock on a shady veranda. It would be my idea of heaven.

The horses were blowing long before we got to the summit of the pass that led to the far reaches of the Bar C land. It was good cattle-grazing country where cows could breed and live wild until rounded up. We saw several bunches of cows with their bulls and calves. They were tame because they had not seen man for a long, long time.

It took two days before we had to move with caution as we neared the mouth of the canyon. The terrain was good, the scenery breathtaking but broody. The Indians began to act spooky. There were rituals and prayers to appease the spirits of the water and of the trees which were now becoming thick on the ground.

The canyon was a long deep gash in the ground with rearing sides overgrown with piñons and junipers and scrub brush interspersed with lush grass and the narrow foaming river boiled in the bottom like a silver snail trail.

I knew this canyon and I knew where the

cabin was located. It should have been just a pile of mouldering logs by now. But it wasn't. It had been rebuilt within the last ten or fifteen years. But it was on the same site.

We drew in the horses and surveyed the tiny cabin from long distance. A thin stream of telltale smoke lifted straight up in the breathless air.

I heard a muttering amongst the Indians, and I knew why, for opposite the cabin was a great round boulder and that boulder was an old Cheyenne sacrificial stone.

It had been desecrated by having a number of lean-to shanties built around it, and a parcel of horses and animals and chickens grazing if my eyes didn't deceive me. No wonder I could feel the anger all around me.

I could imagine the stink of that Noah's ark of a place would have to be sniffed to be believed.

Tom edged closer to me.

'My God, I never dreamed this place had been built up. I stumbled across it once when I was a youth and it was just a pile of junk. Someone must have been living here for years!'

Ned! Now why should I get the notion of Ned living up here? But it figured, and if he did so, then Kate must have known about it.

Again the name Ned conjured up an elusive figure that I couldn't identify. I didn't know his age, why he should loom importantly and why Kate Beamish seemed to figure with him. It was an instinctive spine-crawling feeling I had about her and him. Yeh, my gut feeling was working overtime.

Chief Chocata's pony moved restlessly as he surveyed the scene. I saw why. His knuckles were white as he pulled back hard on the reins, his face grim. He didn't like what he saw.

'Well? What do we do now?' I asked, more to hear myself speak than wanting to ride hell for leather down there committing mayhem. The hate and the revenge were being diluted now as the time came for the reckoning. I was finding out that I was just another old man, bold enough to threaten and spit blood when angry, but when it came time to put action where my mouth was, I was a mite chary.

I concentrated on Jed's death at my hands and Kate bamboozling old Tom into marrying her when she was already married and us boys' ruined lives and the long years I'd dodged the law and worked my butt off to make my own fortune.

I managed to work up a little hate sweat but it was hard work. It had been so long ago. Now it didn't seem so important.

'What do we do?' the chief repeated. 'We wait for Slippery Snake who is down there now. He will tell us how many we face. Soon he will return and then we can make plans.'

'I thought the Cheyenne just charged in yelling and hallooing and trusted to surprise and the approval of the Great Spirit.'

The old chief controlled his dancing pony and he gave me a look that should have split my head open.

'That was in the old days. Now we use our

heads like your military commanders and so save lives. We cannot afford to throw away our young braves' lives any more. Not if we are to survive as a nation in our own right!'

I nodded. I knew what he was getting at. So many of the Cheyenne were now cooped up on the reservation, emasculated, living on handouts and turning into drunken bums. For a proud chief, it was heartbreaking so those who chose to follow him into the wilds, were doubly valuable. They were the fathers of the future and the stud stock of the Cheyenne future.

'Chief, this is a great thing you do at this time. You have made our trouble, your trouble.' I glanced over at young Tom who was raking the log cabin with his binoculars for signs of life apart from the smoke. I gestured to him. 'Tom Coggins will always be indebted to you for help today.'

The chief regarded me gravely.

'It is not only for him. Those men down there have insulted and desecrated our most sacred place, also made a mockery of our beliefs and of our gods. As true Cheyenne, we cannot let this happen.'

'Very well. I think holing-up down there was the most unsafe place that Joshua and his followers could choose. I am surprised that Mrs Coggins did not make them aware of the danger!'

The old chief snorted.

'The old woman chief cares nothing for Indians and knows nothing of our way of life. She regards us as vermin and less valuable than her horses. We have no right to exist. She sees the land as hers. We are the interlopers, not her and her kind! Now we teach her a lesson!'

It sounded bad for Kate, and I sure wouldn't lift a finger for her, what with the chief gunning for her, and her own son...

Tom put away his binoculars and edged close, his face grim.

'She's down there right enough,' he grated. 'Like a fool I was hoping...' He bit his lips and turned away. I hawked and spat to hide a sudden emotion. It was strange. No other man excepting Jed had ever meant much to me. What hurt Tom, hurt me.

I was being broody and waiting for Slippery Snake wasn't helping any. I think I should have preferred blundering in and trusting to surprise and getting the unpleasant bits over with.

Then suddenly it was all go. Slippery Snake was talking at the chief's side and waving his arms and looking plumb excited.

It appeared that a new member had ridden in the night before and my mind flew to the mysterious Ned. Slippery Snake had counted all the numbers of the fingers of his hands, so that there was around eight or ten counting Kate. We were going to have a regular little battle on our hands.

I listened to Tom and the chief argue the toss about how they should set about mopping them up and Tom sounded more savage than Chocata.

For a mild man, Tom was sure bitten deep with hate.

I watched him. I think he was a mite crazy

at this time. He'd been drinking too, something he wasn't prone to do in normal conditions. I kept silent, but I was determined that he shouldn't be the one to kill his mother, if she had to be killed...

Then, it was time to go on the offensive and it was then Chief Chocata lived up to his name as great chief. He'd sure studied those Washington generals' tactics for he deployed half his men to go in close on their bellies. The rest went in on horseback on a charge more to surprise and paralyse than to kill.

So it was, that I found myself charging downhill with a bunch of Indians for the first and last time in my life and circling that noisome shack and yelling fit to bust like any red man.

We must have put the fear of God up those inside, for we'd circled them and were starting another round before the first sign of life. I guess they were pretty confident of themselves for they had no lookout and we'd caught them having chow, because as we circled I got a distinct sniff of roast beef.

We were well away from the shack and moving targets so that though slugs whistled past like hornets, there were no casualties. I did a bit of half-hearted firing, at no target in particular. I was uncomfortable because of the Indians. It didn't seem right, horsing in like savages.

But I got a right shock. I forgot the snake-belly brigade and suddenly all was confusion and a-screaming and a-yelling and burning brands were being thrown on the roof of the tinder-dry cabin.

I pulled up with horror. Of course I could see that the horse brigade had only been a diversion while the most skilful braves moved in and fired the place. I cursed. It was one thing going in trading shots, but this sneaky business of putting all to the torch was too much like massacre.

I looked for Tom. How would he contemplate living easy if his ma fried to death?

But Tom was nowhere to be seen. So I dragged on the reins and took refuge under a cottonwood and watched.

The roof was blazing now and suddenly the door burst open and a wild-eyed man ran out with his hands up. An explosion and the man was blown apart.

It was then I dug my heels in and my horse leapt forward and I was charging Chief Chocata who was deliberately taking aim and waiting for the next victim to come out. But the first man's fate was momentarily putting a hitch in the proceedings.

Suddenly there was a volley of bullets fanning out from broken windows and two braves lined up beside Chocata were flung from their ponies.

Then a figure loomed in the doorway and Chocata, raging and wild, pulled the trigger and missed the darting figure and I lunged forward at the same moment to deflect the gun.

'Stop it!' I thundered. 'Let them come out! There's a woman in there, remember!'

Chief Chocata gave me a strange look but backed his horse and then turned and swiftly galloped away, a dignified but affronted chief. I watched him go, regretful but relieved. It hadn't been good business to implicate the Cheyenne into this affair.

Thinking on those lines, I quite forgot the location and why Chief Chocata had joined us.

I manoeuvred myself so that I was before the open door. Now flames were glowing orange on the inside.

'All of you come out with your hands up,' I roared and wondered whether the words would be heard over the crackle of the flames. I shouted again and this time, Kate was pushed out first and her body covered the little man behind her. The old bastard was not taking chances.

Kate was blackened and coughing hard, her white hair awry and her face pinched as if all the old Adam was frightened out of her.

'Come on, hurry, all out, damn your hides and no funny stuff. There's guns on you from all angles. The first wrong move and you get it.'

I sounded a lot tougher than I was. I was shaking inside. This wasn't old man's business but as Tom wasn't around, someone had to take charge.

I watched those inside tumble through the door like chickens with a fox after them. They coughed and spluttered and were no danger to us. The braves on ponies watched them impassively while several young bucks overstepped their enthusiasm by throwing more burning brands into the shack that was now burning with a menacing roar.

I watched the huddled scorched figures and then realized the big man, Joshua was missing. It didn't seem in character for him not to be first man out. Maybe he'd been wounded in the first rush. Somehow I was relieved that he at least was out of it. He was the wily bastard who might have stiffened the others' backbones.

I motioned them all back and the Indians closed in and I saw that they too had their own plans for them.

They were herded into a corral and ringed by strangely silent braves. I saw the little runt whom Kate said was her husband and he was talking to a stranger, who must be the Ned who had broken out of jail. It was ironic. It wasn't a time for joking, or I might have laughed. It was a case of jumping out of the pot and into the fire!

Ned was a much bigger guy than Kate's runt who might have been taller if he hadn't been bandy-legged. This man was broad built and had powerful shoulders, no doubt developed from years of breaking stone. He was heavily bearded and from what I could see, a man with confidence and leadership. Of all of them, he would be the most dangerous. His manner reminded me of someone but I couldn't put a finger on it. All I knew, was that in the present dire straits he was in, he wasn't panicked, downbeat or finished. Not like the rest of them who sat about with heads down and the very picture of despair.

There was one thing for sure. Neither of them appeared worried about old Kate. She sat alone, staring straight ahead and as if she wasn't really part of all this. At that moment she was just another old woman who wouldn't say boo to a goose.

But I knew different.

I was contemplating getting her into some kind of shelter away from the sun. It would have to be one of the small shacks built around the boulder but they would be smelly, bug-ridden and squelchy from animal shit.

Then I saw that the Indians were systematically firing these stench-huts and that the boulder was surrounded by what one might describe as a funeral pyre. It was one way of purifying their sacred place. I could understand that.

Chief Chocata was watching the proceedings, immobile on his pony, his hands stretched high in the air as if he prayed and supplicated help from the Great Spirit.

I hoped he would get what he wanted or resentment of white marauders might spill over at some future time. It was Ripple, I kept reminding myself, that made him sweet to all at the Bar C.

I had made my mind up to take Kate away from the press of prisoners and braves, when Tom came galloping back from wherever he had been.

He slid to a halt beside me, his face white and bloodied. I saw he had a nasty graze on the side of the head. Evidently he would never be so near a bullet that hadn't his name on, again.

'Where the hell have you been? Your ma's in the middle of that lot. I was just going to get her out.'

'Why? Let the old bitch stay where she is!'

Tom's voice was implacable.

'But she's your ma, Tom,' I said weakly.

'Bullshit! What does that really mean? Not damn much by the way she treated me. Let her suffer, I say!'

I was silent. Tom seemed to have changed. There was iron in him. Then I asked him again.

'Where've you been?'

'Chasing that blasted Joshua. Did you

know he got away?'

I cursed. I really thought he'd died in that inferno.

'Hell! When…?'

'When we were pussy-footing about. I found one of the snake-belliers stabbed in the back. Chocata's grandson was with me and we followed his trail. The bastard had got himself a horse and we followed quite easy. Then he caught Little Bear unawares, blasted his head off and I had to take cover. I had him holed-up for quite a time, then he out-smarted me by bellying up behind me.' He fingered the blood smear on his head. 'I'm lucky I'm here. He winged me and I tumbled down a-ways and knocked myself out. He didn't come to see if I was dead or alive. The tumble must have convinced him I was finished.'

'So he got away?'

'Yeh. I don't know how long I was out, but it took plenty long enough to get back here. What's happening now?'

'I have a sneaky idea that Chief Chocata is

going to hold a tribunal and we're not going to have any say in the matter!'

'Looks mighty like it. You know how touchy Indians are about their sacred places.'

Tom looked broodingly in the direction of his mother.

'I suppose in the circumstances I should talk to her.' He didn't sound too enthusiastic about the prospect.

'I'll go get her,' I said swiftly before he could change his mind.

But I had a job persuading Chocata. He wanted her there under his eye. There must have been a mighty lot of resentment building up against her all these years. I kept quiet about Little Bear.

'But she's Tom Coggins's mother after all, Chief.' I wondered why I should beg so hard for the old witch.

The chief was slow in considering. Clearly that argument didn't really wash with him. Then he said slowly, 'She can't run away. Her old legs wouldn't get her far. You may take her, but you will be responsible for her.

When we are ready she will return to be with the others to be tried and sentenced...'

I gulped. It didn't sound too good for those guys sitting huddled together under the watchful eyes of the Cheyenne.

I handed my horse to one of the braves and shouldered my way through the press of bodies ringing the corral. I spoke no word, but held out my hand and hauled her to her feet. Her hand was cold and clammy like that of a corpse. I hated this first touch of the woman who had haunted me for years. I looked at her with curiosity for she was like a burnt-out corpse.

But I was wrong. When I drew her away from the corral and she saw Tom she came back burningly alive. The fires had only been damped down.

'Tom! Get me out of here! There's been a mistake! I was kidnapped.'

'Quit lying, Ma. I know all about the visit to the bank. You were leaving and somehow something's gone wrong. Why, Ma? Why up and leave us?'

Her old face twisted with a venom I never expected to see on a mother's face for her son.

'Why? You prudish, lily-livered apology for a son that a woman was ever saddled with! I'll tell you, why!' She paused to take several deep breaths as if all the hate inside her was eating up her lungs like acid. Tom had gone white.

'You and your pa were nothing in my life.' Her bosom heaved with the pent-up hatred of years. 'Tom Coggins was a means to an end. I never meant to stay all the long years I rotted away at the Bar C! I hated every damn year of it, and you,' – turning to Tom – 'helped to keep me there.'

'But Ma...'

'Shut up while I tell it while I'm in the mood! Tom died and I was free to run the Bar C, which made up for the situation I was in. But there was Pete, my husband, in jail for life. My handsome, gambling Pete who had the Midas touch and lost it. And I was a wanted woman, accused of helping to set up a killing.'

'But how? How could a woman like you set anyone up?' Tom's tone was anguished.

Kate laughed that reckless laugh that reminded me of the Kate Jed and I knew all those years ago.

'Because, my prudish good-living son, I was madam in my husband's whorehouse and in that business it is easy to set up any man anytime. But I didn't figure on one of the whores betraying us, and neither did Pete. So, the whorehouse was raided. I fled on the first train out of San Francisco and came to Abilene.'

She hesitated and I saw her delve deep into the past and what she saw, hurt. Then she flung up her head, the old courage that had sustained her so long, apparent.

'I left my son Ned, behind. He was only five years old. The nurse who looked after him had taken him away to protect him when the trouble started. I never saw him again until he was a man. They put my lovely boy into a charity home and nearly worked him to death. But when he was old enough, he ran away.'

Tom was silent, white and sick-looking. I guess his ma's past and the news he had a half-brother was churning him up something real bad. I asked the inevitable question.

'What happened to him?'

'What do you think happened?' Her tone was strident, defiant. 'He lived on his wits like his father and finished up inside and one time even broke rock alongside his pa.'

'Why didn't your old man swing?'

'Because he spent all our loose cash on a bent lawyer.'

'How come you still have property from that time?'

She gave a great start and Tom slowly raised his head and looked at her. This was news to him.

The time was long gone to protect that boy from his ma. Now was the time he had to cut all ties. He had to know the truth.

'Your husband didn't use all your spare cash on his lawyer. You invested five thousand dollars in another whorehouse and later you acquired, and I quote from a source very reliable and accurate, several lucrative businesses; namely a milliner's shop, a grocery and liquor store, a saloon and a boarding-house, all managed separately so that none complicated the rest. Am I right, Kate?'

She took a deep shuddering breath.

'Yes.'

Tom made as to hurl himself at her. I grabbed him and he nearly jerked my arms out their sockets but I held him.

'You old bitch! You watched while I worked and slaved, and worried my guts out that we were done! You let me go and humiliate myself by having to ask a stranger for help!' He looked wildly round as I struggled with him.

'Easy, boy, easy!' He flung me off.

'I suppose you were saving your cursed cash for your other son, God damn him!'

She thrust her chin out, lips tight.

'You had a good start. You lived easy on the ranch. You had it given you. Ned needed a new start. I wanted him out of the pen with a stake to start again somewhere else where he wasn't known. Is that so bad for a mother to want that?'

'Then why not give it to him when he first came out of jail? He's been coming here for years, hasn't he?'

Kate had the grace to flush. Now she grew angry.

'The first time I saw him again he was twenty and he was wild and suspicious of me. He accused me of abandoning him. I gave him cash to start again but it wasn't any good. He needed the excitement, the living on a knife edge. He laughed at me, but when he was down and out, he would blackmail me … I told him where to hide out and I made the excuse that we were struggling to survive. *I wasn't going to let him squander the cash or the properties I'd sacrificed myself for over the years!* He could have had it all, if he would have gone straight.' She raised her head and looked at Tom, her mouth twisting in bitter irony. 'If he'd been more like you...'

Tom turned his back on her, his head back, staring at the sky.

'But why treat me like a dog? I've never understood you. You never welcomed Amy and you can't stand your own grand-children. Why, for God's sake?'

'Because I never wanted you. You were thrust upon me. If it wasn't for you, I should never have married Coggins! I should have made a new life for myself until such time I could get Pete out of jail. I would have found a way!'

'But...' – I scratched my head, bewildered, – 'old Tom was Tom's pa...' I was being bloody dim.

Tom whirled about and pointed accusingly at Kate.

'You're telling us that I'm not Tom Coggins's son?'

I found myself holding my breath and you could have cut the silence with a knife. She closed her eyes.

Memories were tumbling around in my brain. I was remembering Jed and him being mesmerized with her. Jed? Was he young Tom's father? Hell! I'd known Jed through and through; if there had been the least likelihood, I should have known.

The woman was just confusing the issue. I'd got it all panned out. You couldn't believe a word the bitch said. She was wriggling like a fish caught on a hook. I never got to the why and wherefore of it all because she suddenly screamed at Tom.

'Don't you see it? Are you so blind that you can't see what's under your nose?'

It's a wonder those braves watching the prisoners didn't hear our jaws drop.

Tom looked at me. I was still digesting her words like a dim-witted fool.

'You mean, he's…?'

She laughed wildly.

'Yes, you stupid oaf! Ask him. Ask him if we didn't couple like a pair of rutting dogs!'

The words rang hard and clear and I remembered that coupling and I remembered the guilt afterwards. Then it hit me. She'd deprived me of my own son as well as all the rest.

I choked and this time it was Tom who held me back from striking her.

He had his arm about my shoulders. I felt the invisible bond of kinship. Something I had sensed but hadn't recognized before.

The thought of the lost years seemed to send me crazy for a while or maybe it was the shock and the hate for the woman who could do this thing.

Then gradually I came to realize that the sweet Amy was my very own daughter-in-law and that her children were my very own grandchildren. Grandchildren I never expected to have.

And all the time the black-hearted bitch sat and watched my agony with bitter amusement. I hoped she would rot in hell!

# EIGHT

It took two days before Chief Chocata was satisfied that the sacred site was purified and that the rest of the proceedings could start.

Campfires had been lit at a respectful distance from the great rock. The prisoners were baited for amusement, but fed and only one, who foolishly retaliated, got shot.

There was a beating of drums in the distance. Faint but sinister, they went on all night and all day and even for us, they tightened nerves and encouraged any aggression within us.

Then the drums beat louder. It was a signal and a picked team of young bucks heaped up the fire that had been tended but not used for cooking, in front of the great boulder.

Then when the flames were spiralling high and throwing off an orange glow in the darkness, the youths started their dance.

I had never watched a ceremonial dance but had heard of such and how impressive they were. Chief Chocata was in charge of the ceremony and I realized that he was also their Medicine Man.

I hoped he would remember when he worked himself up into a frenzy that we were friends of his. If he and the young bucks got carried away, then there'd be a present-day massacre and we shouldn't be able to do anything about it.

Kate was now back in the ring of prisoners. The chief was not dishing out privileges because she was a woman. I saw her having to relieve herself in public and being hooted and laughed at by the braves who thought it a good joke.

Tom and I sat together. He, poor devil, torn between his disgust and hatred for his ma and his natural horror of what might happen to a woman by the Indians.

I had plenty to think about. If Chief Chocata didn't turn on us, it was going to be a whole new life for me. For the first time, I should have folks to plan for... It made me a little lightheaded.

The drums beat louder and faster, the Indians casting grotesque shadows as they leapt and whirled and hollered. It was head-splitting stuff and my body shook as if I had the ague. The drums beat right inside my head until I couldn't think. I think it was then I collapsed.

I came round to a profound silence. It rang bells in my ears, and I struggled up on one elbow. Where the hell was I, and what was happening?

I was alone.

I crept from the shadows and moved nearer to the glow of orange light. The fire was now only half its size and a thick bed of red ash tinged with grey gave off sparks and puffs of gas and a heat that shimmered.

The prisoners and their guards were removed and were now squatting behind the great boulder. I crept nearer and heard the chief's deep voice haranguing his listeners.

I saw also that old Pete and Ned were stripped and they were both tied to the same stake facing each other and blood dripped from bloody stripes. My eyes sought and found Kate, who huddled on the ground, her head in her hands. I could see she had been forced to watch the punishment. I had a nasty feeling both men were dead. They looked like sides of beef, slack and shapeless.

Chief Chocata was being fair or as fair as an Indian could be. The rest of the gang who were regarded as followers were stripped and beaten and then turned out without clothes or horses or guns and told to run.

I wasn't sure whether that was a mercy or not. It might have been to give the eager bucks some hunting practice.

Then I watched as they dragged Kate to stand before them. Two bucks held her upright. I saw that she sagged at the knees. I looked around for Tom and finally found where he was watching and I saw that he too was being restrained. Chief Chocata was making sure he didn't have a change of heart and muck up the judgement.

There was a lot of argy-bargy, accusations and a waving of hands and finger pointing which I couldn't follow. Kate seemed to grow smaller and smaller.

I was beginning to get worked up. It was one thing promising to kill her to myself when I was in a hot-headed humour, and it was something quite different when a menacing bunch of Indians threatened her. A quick bullet would have been satisfactory, but this cold-blooded deliberate torture of what they might do ... was unacceptable. I cursed Chief Chocata. Underneath that friendliness he had shown he was only a bloody savage after all.

They strung her up. Hands and arms stretched so that her old shoulder muscles creaked and she screamed. She endured two lashes and then she fainted.

I moved quickly before I could find reasons why I shouldn't threaten Chocata. I was behind him and holding my gun hard into his side.

'Enough's enough, Chief. This has got to stop, right now. Understand? Right now!'

He looked at me with a dispassionate interest as he had done before. He didn't hate me, but he didn't love me, either. But at that moment I was humiliating him. I dug my gun further into his side and he took the hint.

He raised his hands on high, for he was ever the showman and had to salvage his pride and he rattled off a great long spiel which I at first was suspicious of, and I dug my gun deeper and deeper until he grunted. Then I saw the braves slip away.

'What's happening, Chief?'

He was very dignified.

'I have told them that justice has been done and our mission is accomplished and they are now free to return to their hunting.' His lips twitched and I remembered the poor bastards who had been stripped and sent on their way on foot. 'That is what you wanted?'

I nodded. The crafty bastard was making sure he kept his braves happy!

Within minutes, there wasn't a Cheyenne left around. I watched Chief Chocata leap aboard his pony. For a long moment he faced me and Tom, who had hurried to me when he found his guards gone.

The chief held up his right arm, waving his rifle high in the air as a salute, then wheeling his pony bounded away at a fair lick.

I sighed.

'Thank God that's over. We'd better see to your ma.'

We'd just brought her round and I was cleaning the two bloody stripes on her back and picking out pieces of black cotton embedded from her dress when we were both aware of a horse picking its way slowly and carefully in the light of a half moon.

There was a glint of a gunbarrel and Tom and I froze in squatting positions covering Kate.

There was a long low rumble of laughter that froze the blood.

Kate stirred and tried to lift her head to peer in the direction of the sound.

'Joshua? Is that you, Joshua?' she called weakly, and the newcomer trotted into the light of the dying fire. The horse was doubly laden and my heart iced as I saw the little blonde head slumped against Joshua's fat torso.

He looked around, his expression hidden by a deep-crowned black stetson.

'So, I'm a bit late to help old Pete and Ned. What happened to the other boys? Aha!' as I made a quick movement to stand up and ease my aching legs. 'Be very careful, mister. I don't take kindly to sudden movements. And you too, Coggins, even though you're the old woman's son. I know how she regards you. You'd be no loss!'

I spoke carefully, so as not to upset this renegade.

'The Indians turned them adrift for hunt prey. There's just Kate here, and Tom and myself. What do you reckon to do with Annie here? She's sure well adrift from home.'

I kept my old man's voice all innocent-like. It was like walking on egg-shells.

Joshua caressed the bright hair with a fat hand. I saw the child cringe.

'She's a little beauty, isn't she? A regular first-class little topnotcher, who'd make good money down in Brazil!'

I was conscious of Tom ready to spring. The surge of anger boiling up like something tangible. You could nearly taste it. I gave him a warning nudge and I knew it took all his time to control the urge to throw himself at the smiling dog turd.

'What do you want, Joshua? It's a whole new set-up now that Pete and Ned are dead meat. Whatever they had you now inherit. That bankroll they made Kate withdraw from the bank can now be yours. Why not swop the child for the cash and just keep on riding, pal?'

Joshua's eyes gleamed.

'The bankroll's still around then?'

'Sure. Why shouldn't it be?'

Joshua shrugged.

'The old lady's smart. She could have stashed it.'

Suddenly my heart gave a lurch and missed a beat. Where the hell would it be? We had nothing else to trade for Annie. He had the drop on us. He could get at least one of us, maybe two before we could stop him and Annie could be hit.

Kate started to laugh. It was high-pitched and eerie and I was sure she'd flipped out. It sent icy fingers legging it up and down my spine. I was sure she'd flipped when she giggled.

'You'll never see Pete's bankroll, Joshua. It went up in smoke. It was inside the cabin. Where else would it be?' And she roared as at a joke.

I was appalled. She dropped us clean into the shit and she was acting as if she didn't realize that her own granddaughter was in danger! I daren't look at Tom, so I concentrated on Joshua. I saw the momentary disappointment in his eyes and then he dismounted and when he lifted Annie down she made a dive for her pa and Joshua caught her to him and cuffed her ear.

'Why you bastard...!' Tom sprang, full of fury, tugging frantically at his Colt as he did so.

The stupid fool hadn't a gob of spit's chance on a hot stove of beating him to a draw and he was risking his child into the bargain. I wanted to cuss from arsehole to breakfast time but I held back so's not to complicate matters.

I was expecting the blast of the Colt and it came. Tom jumped back as if pulled by puppet strings and a great splash of red appeared under his shoulder.

I caught him as he arched backwards and his weight brought me to the ground as well.

I found myself looking up at Joshua. I was staring down that black hole in the gun barrel and it was a damn sight too near for my liking. He held the Colt firmly and in his other hand was Annie, too frightened to cry but she was near enough for me to see the tears sparkling, ready to spill over.

I vowed I'd get that fat dung slug if I had to lick his arse beforehand to get Annie away from him. I managed a weak smile.

'Now there's no call to take on, Joshua. Just take it easy, mister. It looks like Tom's finished. Now can't you and me cash in on the situation?'

'What you mean, old man?'

'Well, look at it this way. There's only you and me and that crazy old woman knows what's happened here. I can make things easy for you. You could go legit. Nobody's going to connect you with this tarradiddle, especially if it's known you're my new partner. What do you say to that?'

Joshua looked at me suspiciously.

'Why should you do anything for me?'

'In exchange for the child. There's bound to be an uproar about her going missing. She's going to be an embarrassment to you. You'd never get her undetected to Brazil. That would be a crazy idea.'

Joshua grinned.

'I never meant for her to go to Brazil. I'd sell her to one of the Mexican cathouses. A little blonde would go down a treat.'

'You would still have to run the risk of being caught slave trafficking. You know what a hooha there is nowadays if a man's caught selling kids.'

Joshua shrugged.

'What's a trip inside anyway? It's worth a gamble. Blondes make good money.'

'Not little 'uns like her. They'd have to wait too long before they could use her.'

'Not that long. They break 'em in early over the border.'

I was beginning to sweat heavy. Joshua obviously had a price in mind.

'It's more than just a stretch in the pen. Nowadays slavery is a hanging offence.'

That made Joshua stop and think. He took a half-empty bottle of whiskey from his jerkin pocket and took a swig while he considered like. He nodded. Thank God he agreed with me about that. He took another long swig and burped. I was beginning to think he was well shot. Joshua was a man who could take his liquor and not look affected, but I suspected he was at the stage when he could go berserk or turn maudlin.

He didn't do either. He bawled for food and I indicated a forgotten pot left by the Indians which contained dubious stew.

I thought I might catch him unawares but the bastard was cute. He kept Annie near him and he fastened her to him with his bandanna and then kept a wary eye on Kate and me.

I eyed Tom with concern. But he did not stir and I didn't want Joshua to take an interest in him for if he was still alive the fat man was tanked up enough to kill Tom in cold blood.

As far as I was concerned, I was still treading daintily on egg-shells.

I waited until Joshua cleared the pot. He might be in a more amenable mood for a trade. I moved a little to be nearer Tom because like a fool I'd laid down my gun earlier with the idea of oiling and cleaning it. It had been forgotten about in the flurry of Joshua coming upon us unawares with Annie seated in front of him.

Kate made a bit of a diversion by suddenly sitting upright. She looked distinctly flipped over, her eyes stared and her cheeks were sunken. Also her mouth was still twisted and now I was realizing that her earlier rage must have brought on a stroke. Then she keeled over and was clawing the ground until the tips of her fingers were tinged with blood. Spittle oozed from her mouth and her mouth went slack. She was an awesome sight, a caricature of her former self.

Joshua nodded in her direction.

'Shut her up, old man, or do you want me to put a bullet in her? I wouldn't let my pet dog live like that.'

I moved nearer to her and took her hands to still them.

'Kate? Can you hear me? Kate, it's all right. Just be still.'

She stared at me uncomprehending and I knew that fear had finally conquered the strong-willed woman, as man had never done.

'Kate?' I tried again but it was no use. She didn't know me. She was just a quivering lump of meat with the brain burnt out.

I turned my attention again on Joshua. He was stroking Annie's head and smiling horribly at her and it gave me a jolt.

I was her only hope and I had to play my cards right.

Then Annie cried and Joshua lost patience and slapped her again.

Suddenly I was aware of Tom who was awake. His face was pinched and white. He'd lost a whole heap of blood. But all his attention was on the two guns, his and mine, that had been thrown carelessly down.

I couldn't even remember how many shots were in the chambers of my own. I certainly hadn't loaded up because of the intention of cleaning and oiling them. I knew too, that Tom would be in much the same shape.

The only thing was to go with the charade of pretending to offer a partnership, until such time as an opportunity should occur. It was going to be a matter of wits and I wasn't very sure of myself.

But I had to win this battle of wits, for Annie's sake. I just *had* to. I had no choice.

I took the plunge and started in again. Joshua was looking more relaxed with having a full belly. Maybe, the mention of hanging might have given him food for thought.

'Well, what about it? Have you considered my offer? It means far more than you know, mister. I've got considerable influence back in Chicago and I can put my hands on more cash then you'll ever see in your lifetime. Don't you understand? You could travel anywhere in the world. You could visit Paris, France, or London, England or anywhere and have the best food and drink and what's more important still, the prettiest women. They'd be licking your hands, kissing your arse because of the cash you could toss around. You can also gamble in Monte Carlo, be someone special. How about it?'

'You paint a mighty fine picture, mister,

and I'm nearly tempted, but that kind of stuff isn't for me. I'm a very plain man.'

I sighed inwardly. Of all the awkward devil-cursed turds a man could come across! He sure was a miserable barrel of shit!

'Well, what would it take to make you happy?'

Joshua took on the puzzled look of a man with the sozzled brains of a gnat.

'I don't know, maybe having plenty to drink, a different girl every night and a bank just begging to be robbed!' He grinned. 'Now that would be something, especially if it was open season on banks!'

'You would rather steal it than spend your own bankroll all legit?'

'Yeh, why not? I wouldn't care what happened to money I stole. If it was mine, I'd hang on to it! Yeh, that's right. I'm only comfortable spending what isn't mine!'

'Jesus bloody wept! You mean you *like* your present life?'

'Yeh, why not? It's exciting. Mind you, I get pissed off when my buddies catch it, like as now. But there'll be other buddies. There always has been. No sweat.'

'So, you're turning my offer down. What about Annie?'

Joshua shrugged his wide shoulders.

'I'll take my chances with her.' And he grinned showing yellow twisty teeth amidst a regular forest of bristly hair.

'So that's your last word?'

'Yep! I think I'll keep her as my ace in the hole.

I rolled over and grabbed my gun and he lunged kicking out and Annie was dragged to the ground. He cursed as he clawed his own weapon. I fired a ragged shot but missed and I was lying looking again into the barrel of his gun as he deliberately took aim.

This was it. I'd gambled and lost. It didn't matter which way I rolled. It would be like shooting a cornered rat. I didn't have a chance...

Then a rifle cracked and I saw the surprised look on his face before he tottered and fell away from Annie who lay quivering and crying alongside him.

I don't remember what happened just after that. I think I must have done something silly, like fainting. The only excuse I could think of afterwards was that I'm an old man and excused any stupid reactions...

## NINE

Someone was slapping my face quite hard. It hurt. I opened my eyes to protest and found myself looking into an incredible pair of brown eyes of an unusual liquid beauty. I was a mite confused and it was another half-minute before I recognized Ripple.

I was never so glad to see anyone in my life!

She supported me as I sat up shakily.

'What happened?'

She smiled and it was a pretty sight to see. She looked around and I followed suit and saw another pretty sight ... a whole mess of law-abiding cowboys with a sprinkling of townsfolk and best of all, Amy, sat close to the embers of the fire cuddling Annie as if she would never let her go again, and beside her, propped up against a saddle was Tom, shirtless, but wearing a broad white bandage covering his shoulder and his ribs.

I wanted to shout Hallelujah! and keep on shouting it. By cripes, I'd suffered wondering whether that boy was still with us! He could have bled to death.

Suddenly everything was going black and I was hard put to breathe and Ripple was doing things fast like putting my head down between my legs and then thumping me to make me gasp. It did the trick and then she held a bottle to my mouth and I felt the bite of liquor in my guts.

I took a second swipe and that put me to rights. I coughed and snorted phlegm, then stretched and I dragged myself upright and staggered across to Amy and Tom.

There was tears in my eyes when I hunkered down beside them.

'By God, I've never been so pleased to see anyone in my life.' I grinned like a fool kid sassing up his first girl.

She raised her head and it was then I saw the ravages of the last few days. She looked at least ten years older. It was going to take a hell of a lot of putting behind her.

'Thank you for buying time for Annie. Tom's told me about it and how he couldn't move but he could listen. He said it was a nightmare...' She shuddered. 'If that man had got away with Annie, we might never have caught up with him. I can't bear to think what might have happened.' Her body trembled as fresh tears came.

Tom put an awkward arm about her. He was mighty weak and sore. It was going to take time before he was a well man again.

I looked about me and saw the marshal talking to Kate who was huddled well apart from the newcomers. At least I say talking. He was more like listening to a crazy woman raving for her mouth was going constant.

There were those within hearing pitch who appeared avidly interested. The Coggins family was going to make rare scandal meat for the next few weeks.

As I said before, I didn't take to the marshal but I suppose he was a good man in his own way. He was certainly better in town than out in the open. I had the feeling he didn't set much store in having to arrange posses and go chasing hell for leather over unknown terrain catching up with renegades and cattle rustlers. His idea of managing his town was to lounge in his jail with his feet on his desk with a jar of coffee at his elbow and a spittoon within range. And as for the way he walked over to us now, his arse was sore, so I concluded that his main exercise was walking along Main Street twice a day airing his badge and nodding to the business folk of Abilene.

I watched interestedly as he joined us at the miserable remains of the fire. I saw that two of his deputies flanked Kate. Rigby was taking no chances there.

He inclined his head towards her.

'How long has she been in that state, Mr Williams?'

I did a bit of slow reckoning. He could wait my time for an answer. He hawked and spat away from Amy as he waited impatiently.

Then he frowned and scratched the back of his head. His greasy wide-brimmed hat giving him a rash. It was plain to be seen as he bared his head. I think it was a sweat rash. Mind you, it might have been lice, when I come to think of it. He wasn't a very particular kind of man. For a townsman he had quite a smell....

Then I thought it was time I said something.

'An … now … as best as I can recall, it was maybe before she was took off. She says she was kidnapped.'

Rigby snorted.

'Like hell! She doesn't give the same story twice!'

I shrugged my aching shoulders.

'Have it your way, Marshal. Why ask me if you know all the answers?'

Marshal Rigby breathed heavily through his somewhat bulbous nose.

'Now look here, smart arse. You can see by the numbers how we put ourselves out for Mrs Coggins and come a-looking for her little girl. We put ourselves to considerable hardship on the double. Now I reckon you owes us both respect and all the help you can give us as regards this here situation.'

I still didn't know just how much Tom wanted making public. After all, he was the one who would now have to take the gossip, the criticism and the malice that always followed ranchers who managed to make headway in a hard won world. I remained silent.

Tom roused himself and I was relieved. Kate was his mother and it was up to him to co-operate with Rigby.

'Look, Marshal, you did a good job and by God, I'll always be in your debt! You can count on me to back you up, any time.'

Hell! I thought to myself, he wants to be careful there. Rash promises often bounce back! But it wasn't my business...

'Well now, Coggins, I'll have to write a report. I'll also have to have a look through my flyers and see if any of the deceased are wanted. If so, there'll be a reward.'

*'No!'* there was a sudden scream from Kate and we all looked as she struggled like a wildcat to free herself from the two deputies. Those two poor bastards were being respectful because she was a woman and because she was Kate Beamish Coggins, one-time rancher with influence in the community, and both deputies had grown up under her shadow.

Their efforts at holding her were half-hearted and she wrenched herself free and she came storming over, tottering as if she'd drunk half a bottle of bourbon.

'Bastard!' she hissed at a startled Rigby. 'No one's going to cash in on anyone, especially my Pete and Ned! This is a private affair, Marshal, so keep your ugly face out of Coggins business!'

For a moment the marshal looked puzzled. He looked from Kate to Tom and then as a last resort to me.

'What's this about Pete and Ned? I thought we were dealing with that fat bastard who kidnapped Annie Coggins?'

Tom struggled to his feet and faced his ma.

'Go on, Ma, you might as well tell it all, the whole damn rotten business! You're busting to spill it, so get on with it!'

They stood glaring at each other until Tom turned tiredly away.

Kate's head swayed from side to side like a cornered animal. I couldn't believe that this creature was the woman who'd fascinated me against my better judgement all those years ago. I was having a fit of the horrors. It was as if the long years of bitterness, hatred, frustration and grief had eaten into her very body as well as her soul and now all the outward veneer was being stripped away leaving her as she really was.

Her hatred surrounded her like a living pulsating balloon of poisonous gas like that the miners disturbed far down in the depths of the ground which killed. It cut her off from everyone she knew. Her soul was now in an eternal void....

She took a deep quivering breath and then

it all came pouring out, like acid spouting from an over-pressurized bottle.

'You spineless spawn of drunken shit!' She spat at Tom and then she cast me a look that should have struck me dead, pronto. It made the gorge rise in me so that my brain was on fire. To think I had been haunted by thought of her for years. 'Did you ever think that I ever regarded you as my child? You were a curse thrust upon me so that I was trapped by that old slavering fumbler you called a father! I hated you because of what you were and what you did to me. You were a pale ghost of my beautiful aggressive boy who was out there somewhere without his ma! You had what he should have had and I grudged every mouthful of food, every advantage you had and the fact you had a father to love. How do you think I felt when you and your father spent days together and I was alone? The very sight of you was a torment!' I saw Tom flinch as if he was being whipped. The cracked old voice went relentlessly on. 'You ... you puny whiny little bastard who couldn't stand the calf branding! Who shamed me before the hands who sniggered behind my back that I'd given birth to a spineless thing without balls!'

Tom lunged at her but Rigby caught him and pushed him roughly back from Kate. Tom bowed his head and covered his eyes and shuddered before looking at her again.

'I tried to love you. God knows how I tried! I couldn't understand why you couldn't bear to even touch me! You undermined every thought and action I had. You poisoned every impulse I ever had! You sucked the life out of me...'

'There was no life to suck! You were just a skinny lump of nothing! And there you were, old Tom Coggins's heir and he thought the sun shone out of your arse!'

'Why didn't you just go away and leave us? You didn't have to stay!'

There was a long moment and then Kate threw her head back and I knew what she was about to say would devastate her son.

'Because I hoped you would die! You were

a muling puling thing. If you'd died, then the ranch was mine outright and somehow, sometime I would seek out my Ned and everything would be fine. But it didn't happen that way!' And now her voice rose to a shriek.

It was shocking. Those that listened could sense the disillusion, the mortal agony of a proud woman who suffered so much for a lifelong goal that had no chance in reality of being fulfilled. Something she'd sacrificed a son for and the love and respect for his subsequent family. She had sacrificed love for a maggot of an idea and known nothing but loneliness and hate. Even little Annie, as young as she was, instinctively avoided her, was frightened of her, and as for her grandsons, they openly flouted her. She could so easily have turned them into monsters...

'Ma, haven't you said enough?' Tom's voice came low, cold and exhausted.

'I haven't even started yet!' she screamed. It was as if it was all there churning round and round in her brain and the pressure there was punching it out. It all had to come or else her overwrought mind would snap altogether.

'Kate! Listen to me.' I was fumbling with words to distract her but she turned to me like a sword thrust.

'Mind your own bloody business.'

'Tom *is* my business. You told me that with your own lips.'

'Aye, I should have told you that years ago when you left me for that stinking Indian slut! You didn't even want me after that one time! But to go back to your Indian squaw was the final insult. I could have killed you, Lofty!'

'So that's why you're so against Indians, especially Indian women.' I searched the firelit gloom for Ripple. She was sitting close behind Amy and was supporting her back while Amy clasped Annie tightly to her. I saw that Annie was now sleeping and thanked God she was spared seeing the spectacle of her raving grandmother.

Kate laughed.

'Don't get it into your head I was heart broken because you left me. No one could take Pete's place. That little runt brought me alive! He was some man in his heyday. A very different man to the man who came out of the pen. I had his image before me for years. It kept me going when I had to despoil myself by living with a disgusting old man who had ideas in his head but nowhere else! What with him and the daily torture of watching a sickening snivelling brat grow into a yellow-streaked man was nearly too much!'

'That's a lie! Tom was never yellow-streaked!' Amy thrust the sleeping Annie on to Ripple's lap.

Kate looked at her for the first time, with contempt.

'What would you know about it? You've got no guts yourself. The pair of you aren't worth the shit you pass!'

'You're wrong about Tom. He's kind and sensitive and he likes fair play. You're the one who has it all wrong. You're seeing him from your own twisted point of view. You couldn't bear him to be right in anything! You're so rotten inside, that you corrupt even your own thinking. I'm sorry for you, Mrs Coggins, you don't know how sorry.'

'Why you miserable little noddlehead, how dare you be sorry for me?'

'Because you're so alone. Because you're in a limbo of your own making! I'm not a hating woman, Mrs Coggins, but you taught me to hate you. I loathe you, do you understand that? When I married Tom, I thought it would only be a matter of time before we could become good friends. I'd never encountered hate before, not the living breathing kind that you conjured up and made into a real soul-destroying entity. You're evil, Mrs Coggins, and may the Lord have mercy on you for I never shall!'

Kate lunged at her, her hands extended like claws. Amy rolled away from her and then scrambled to her feet hampered by her skirts. She stumbled and Kate went after her before any of us men who were watching and listening fascinated, could move a muscle.

Kate caught Amy's cheek, drawing blood. Amy gasped, and then swooped and twisted round, skirts flaring about her. There was a glint in the dim light and then I saw what Amy had swooped for. She was holding Tom's gun before her and pointing straight for Kate's heart.

'God forgive me for what I do now, but it has to be done!'

I tried to get to her. She was going to do the job I'd set for myself. I should be the one to put Kate down like a rabid dog.

I was too late.

The gun went off with an ear-shattering explosion so close that we could smell the powder burns.

Kate's chest disintegrated into a red circle of blood which spewed like a great star.

I heard the weapon drop and then after a moment or two which seemed like aeons of time I heard Annie cry.

Tom caught Amy as she fainted.

And that was how it was.

Well, I've got it all writ down. It's been a hard job what with the writing of it for my old stiff fingers have not been used to a lot of pen-pushing. Also because of the feelings all this has brought back.

It all had to be writ proper so that the circuit judge can read it all for himself and make a fair and just assessment.

There's going to be a rare old howdy-do when it all comes out. God knows it won't be kept quiet. The newspapers will thank us for all the extra reading that will be done.

All I can now say is that Amy was taken by Marshal Rigby to the jail and charged with murder. She was kept in that poky place for more than a week until the townsfolk of Abilene rose up and said it was a disgrace her being inside with a lot of stinking cowboys.

So she was allowed home, which was a Godsend for Tom and the children who were pining for her.

It seems we have to wait another couple of months before the circuit judge arrives for the trial. In the meantime I got Saltash on the job and we have a lawyer coming from San Francisco for fear there might be trouble.

But I don't think there will be trouble. Kate wasn't the one for making friends. Most folk think Amy did right in doing what she did. Amy herself however, has never quite got over what she was driven to do. She's convinced that Saint Peter won't let her through the Pearly Gates when her time comes.

She spends most of her time when she isn't looking after the kids with Ripple's help, with her head in the Bible and quoting dire warnings to anybody who will listen.

I'm staying permanent at the Bar C nowadays. It's ironic really. I could have shared the place with Jed if things hadn't gone wrong.

Still, I'm there now, and I've got my own rocking chair on the veranda and the boys and Annie come and pester me and I love it.

At least some good's come from all these

sad events. I love Amy as my own daughter and as for Tom ... I can never see him as a snivelling brat. I'm proud of him and I'm proud to be his pa.

We get on well. Saltash, although a little bastard at times is a good manager and he's now looking after my interests in Chicago. I'm now living free and easy.

As for Kate's golden mountain and all her hard-won property, it all came to Tom and if she knew, she'd make herself dizzy twisting about in her grave. She wouldn't have been able to stand it.

She's buried in a remote part of the ranch along with her husband and son and I don't think anyone has visited there since we put the last sod down. It's a matter of forgetting about sleeping dogs...

I'm helping Tom to build up the Bar C into the best ranch around and we're starting a new strain of beef and Saltash has been talking about expanding the meat-packing trade down into Puerto Rica, so the sky's the limit.

The only cloud in the sky is Amy's health and her peace of mind. But she's got all our support and our love and if that bloody expensive lawyer knows how to do his job, we can put it all behind us and start again.

So that's it. I'm glad it's finished. I've broken half a dozen pens writing it.

I hear the boys calling me. I've got the job of teaching them how to ride good. They think I'm a hero, and I'd sure as hell never want them to think otherwise.

It's a pity Kate never realized what a gold-mine she had at home ... poor Kate.

The publishers hope that this book has given you enjoyable reading. Large Print Books are especially designed to be as easy to see and hold as possible. If you wish a complete list of our books please ask at your local library or write directly to:

**Dales Large Print Books**
Magna House, Long Preston,
Skipton, North Yorkshire.
BD23 4ND